The Irish Cowboy

D.W. Ulsterman

To Hap,

Perhaps someday further on up the trail...

For all have sinned and fall short of the glory of God.
Romans 3:23

CHAPTER 1

Time had not been kind to Hap Wilkes. His still broad-shouldered back was now bent as a near useless left leg dragged behind him. That leg was not only an unrelenting reminder of the stroke that almost killed him nearly two years ago, but a reminder as well of the emotional pain for things he wished to be undone but could never be. A failing body is something many can navigate but a failed soul is too often a wreck beyond repair.

The man Savage, Montana locals had long called the Irish cowboy never asked for release from his suffering. Instead, he woke up shortly after dawn each morning and welcomed that suffering, took it in, and used it as penance for his sins, grunting from the discomfort and fatigue of a physical shell corrupted by years of hard work and general neglect as he pushed himself out of the same bed he had slept in for most of his nearly eighty years of life.

It was the same bed January died in a decade earlier, the cancer eating at her until nothing but a dried-out husk more nightmare than woman was all that remained. Hap still kept January's side of the bed untouched since the day they took her body out of their small bedroom. January was gone and someday soon he would be as well. If the world took any notice at all it would probably say little more than good riddance to a mean old son-of-a-bitch whose personal shame and simmering resentment made him the kind of company fewer and fewer cared to have around.

That was fine by Hap. He never bothered much with people and their phony pretense. All that wide-eyed grinning and pretending at one another while silently wondering when the other person would just shut up. Since January's death, with the sole exception of taking the thirty-minute drive to Sunday service at St. Michael's, Hap would go weeks or even months without hearing another human being. Instead, his thoughts and attention focused on the feeding and watering of what few domestic animals remained on the ranch and watching over the wild horse herd that had made the Wilkes' property their home for as long as the family had lived there.

There were very few things left in this world Hap loved, but those horses were among them. Last spring, he counted seventy-three of the beautiful creatures, including four new foals. He hoped for a similar number of birthings this spring. They were powerful and proud creatures much like Hap had once been.

Memory can be a terrible thing.

The horses were out there somewhere, possibly grazing in the grass fields on the north side of Vaughn's Hill, named after Hap's grandfather, the man who made his way to America from Northern Ireland and then over a handful of years across the United States to eastern Montana in 1898 where he purchased the nearly three-hundred-acre property on an owner-held contract. Those wild horses had always been as much a part of the ranch as Hap's family had been and in the old Irish cowboy's heart, he felt a kinship toward them that few human beings during his relatively long life could match.

Now what is this about?

A massive plume of dust followed a vehicle nearly a mile away from where Hap stood in front of his home. He had just returned from the barn where he had watered old mare Peanut and then filled Dog's food bowl that sat in a corner of the little front porch at the entrance to the house. Dog was a medium-sized, short-haired brown and white mutt that had wandered in half-starved last year with several infected gashes marking his neck and sides where the coyotes had tried to make a meal of him. The rancher had taken to calling him "Dog", not wanting to waste time thinking up a different name. Dog didn't seem to mind one bit, responding to the less than creative moniker almost immediately. Like Hap, Dog walked with a noticeable limp, one of his hind legs bent from a broken bone that had healed wrong. Despite that limp he managed to get around the property with considerable speed and strength and looked after Hap as much as Hap looked after him.

The dust cloud grew closer as the white, four-door sedan made its way down the mile-long drive. Though his body was near broken Hap's eyes remained sharp and he easily made out the markings of the Richland County Sheriff's Department logo on the side of the vehicle.

That meant a visit from Sheriff Dillon Potts. Hap considered Sheriff Potts a reasonable enough man so long as the sheriff kept to minding his own business. He had known Dillon's father Stan, also a county sheriff, well enough to call the elder Sheriff Potts a friend some years ago. Hap hadn't spoken to Stan since January's death. Last he heard, Stan Potts was cooped up in a rehabilitation center down in Glendive, recovering from a broken hip after falling in the shower.

Poor bastard. No way I let anyone drag me off to one of those places. Rehabilitation my butt – that's where they send old men to die.

The sheriff's car was just a few hundred yards from where Hap stood on the porch. Dog let out a low, suspicious growl, causing the rancher to glance down at the animal and then grunt his agreement.

"Got that right."

CHAPTER 2

Sheriff Potts saw Hap Wilkes staring at him with the familiar intensity of a man who had lived under the open Montana sky all his life. They were eyes Dillon's father had described to him some years ago as always seeming to warn of an approaching storm, their hazel-green flash like the clap of thunder that was a call to others that they would do well to seek cover.

Though now an old man, Hap had once been considered by most around Savage to be among that area's toughest. He didn't suffer fools and had a well-earned reputation for letting anyone know it. Dillon's father, Stan, who was also someone few would have wanted to tangle with twenty or thirty years earlier, had whispered to Dillon as Hap walked by during Jan Wilkes' funeral, "There goes the toughest man I ever known."

That was ten years ago and as the sheriff pulled his car up to the Wilkes home, he was saddened to see how much older Hap now looked. The stroke had certainly taken its toll, forcing Hap to lean against one of the paint-chipped posts holding up the dilapidated front porch as he continued to glare at the arriving sheriff.

Beyond the stroke was something else, though. Hap had always carried a mystery about him, a sort of invisible yet impenetrable wall from behind which he kept himself hidden. It was a condition beyond his simply being a quiet man. Sheriff Potts had long considered Hap to be a person burdened by some kind of terrible, deep regret. There had been rumors of what that regret might have been many years ago when the sheriff was but a boy, but such talk faded as the tellers of that tale died off and the world stopped caring about the long-ago lives of old men.

Every Sunday, as predictable as the rising of the sun, Hap could be found sitting in the very back of the small Catholic church that had served the Savage community for the last century. The rancher said nothing while he listened to the morning prayer, his mouth drawn downward in a perpetual frown, his eyes seeming to never blink. So too was the rancher's Sunday attire always the same—a dark blue dress shirt under a grey jacket, matching gray slacks, and black dress shoes that were polished to a bright sheen. They were the only other pair of footwear the rancher owned besides his long-worn cowboy boots.

Sheriff Potts casually noted Hap's presence on Sunday while he sat with his own family at the front of the church. By the time the Sheriff and his wife and their two daughters rose to leave Hap was already long gone, driving his rust-battered 1948 Ford pickup back to the ranch and the solitude he so clearly craved.

"Hello there, Mr. Wilkes. I apologize for the unannounced visit, but your phone service was disconnected some time ago."

Hap watched the sheriff as Dog stood next to the rancher doing the same. The sheriff looked down at his feet and then looked up again.

"Anyways, uh, I'm here to let you know the feds have been holding some meetings about your property. Specifically, about those horses that run around out here. Seems there was a study done a few years back and, well, they think there might be an endangered species being harmed by that herd of horses.

6

Apparently, it's some kind of lizard. I don't have all the particulars just yet but they contacted my office saying they were having trouble getting a hold of you so I figured it'd be better if I were the one to come out here and give you the heads-up."

Hap's posture straightened as his eyes flashed the approaching storm Dillon recalled his father describing to him years ago. "Is that what you're doing here, Sheriff? Giving me a heads-up?"

The rancher's voice was a rasping whisper, barely audible, yet somehow easily understood.

"Yes, it is. I figured you would rather have me be the one to show up unannounced rather than a bunch of people from the Bureau of Land Management."

Dog had begun to growl again, the sound mimicking the silent noise coming from Hap's eyes. "You say the feds want to come onto my property?"

Dog's growl grew more intense.

"That's what they intend to do first thing tomorrow morning. They need to take foliage samples, observe the herd, stuff like that."

Hap held his right hand in front of Dog's nose, quieting the animal's growling, then looked back up to continue staring down at the sheriff. He turned and gazed out across his property, clearing his throat as his eyes settled on Vaughn's Hill.

"These feds you mention, the Bureau of Land Management, they have a problem with the horses?"

The sheriff shifted on his feet. "That's right. From what I understand they have concerns about the endangered species around these parts and that those horses are damaging the lizard's natural environment."

Hap removed his tattered cowboy hat and brushed it against his faded blue jeans as he shook his head slowly from side to side.

"I figure them horses and those lizards been sharing that same piece of land out there long before any of us or these feds were ever a speck in God's eye."

Dillon agreed with what the rancher was saying but also knew that where the federal government was concerned, it would do what it wanted, common-sense be damned. "I understand, Mr. Wilkes, but they've completed the initial study and now they intend to walk the property tomorrow and either confirm or deny the need to intervene."

"And just what the hell does *intervene* mean in this situation, Sheriff? This here is *my* land, not theirs."

The sheriff placed his hands on his hips and nodded. "It's the government, and you know, if they think they need to look around that's what they're going to do and there's not really anything we can do to stop it."

The rancher made his way down the two steps of his porch, grimacing each time his left foot bumped across the surface. Despite the lame leg and advanced years, the sheriff realized more than a shadow of that legendary toughness his father had remarked on a decade earlier yet remained within Hap's worn frame.

"I asked you a question, Dillon Potts. Don't you dare try to play politician with me, boy. What do these people mean by intervene? What do they think they can do on *my* property?"

Dillon noted how Hap had addressed him without using the title of sheriff. That omission was no doubt meant as a reminder to him that Hap had known his father long before Dillon had come into the world.

"I was told they will have to relocate the herd and then possibly sell them off."

Hap forced his spine to straighten to his nearly full height of just over six feet and then he spit within inches of Dillon's boots. The rancher's narrowed eyes made clear his outrage at the thought of anyone coming and taking a herd of horses that had made their home on his property since a time when America was still young.

"Like hell they will. You let those feds know that if they step one foot on this property, I'll put them in the dirt. Those horses belong here as much as anyone or anything. You hear me, Dillon Potts? Tell them there's one mean old man with nothing to lose who's willing to blow them all to hell before I see them lay one hand on those horses. You tell them that!"

Sheriff Potts took a step back, realizing he could no longer see Hap's dog. The animal was circling around him.

"I need you to calm down, Mr. Wilkes. Making threats against federal workers who are just doing their job isn't going to make this situation any better. Please move back and call your dog."

Hap shook his head, his deeply lined, sun-worn face a mask of disappointment and disgust. "Boy, you ain't ever gonna be the man your father was or the sheriff he was either. Get off my land. Get off my land and don't you or any of them Bureau of Land Management rats ever think of coming here again. I mean it, boy. You're gonna wake up a whole mess of trouble. You all leave me, my property, and those horses alone."

The dog's growl was now directly behind the sheriff, causing him to move his right hand downward to unholster his weapon. Dillon was shocked at how quickly Hap clamped his hand over his forearm as well as how much power the old rancher still possessed. That grip was as strong as any the sheriff had felt before and certainly stronger than his own.

"No need to be reaching for your shooter. I ain't gonna hurt you. Hell, at my age, there ain't much left for me to hurt but myself. Just relax now and deliver my message to those feds. They are to stay off my land."

Hap's grip relaxed which allowed the sheriff to step back. He knew he had every right to arrest the rancher for assault but also knew doing so would only make him look weak to the community and God forbid if his dad found out. Dillon was up for re-election next year and hauling in an old rancher over some endangered lizard dispute would not win him any votes with the rural voters who made up the majority of Richland County, Montana.

"Don't you ever put your hand on me like that again, Mr. Wilkes. I know you and my old man go way back but I'm the sheriff and I have a responsibility to uphold the laws of this county and its people. I can't have you making threats against me or anyone else."

Hap grunted and then spit toward the sheriff's feet again. "Your responsibility is to do what's right. God help you if you don't believe that. Now get on out of here and let me be."

Dillon shook his head and sighed, knowing there would be no changing Hap's mind on this day. He only hoped he could delay the Bureau of Land Management's scheduled arrival tomorrow. The old rancher would still be too willing to fight. The sheriff knew there was likely at least a rifle or two inside the house and that Hap, like most everyone who lived in and around Savage, would know how to use them.

"I'll have to come out here again, Mr. Wilkes. I promise to try to keep the feds from coming out here so soon but if that's what they decide, and you try to stop them I'll have no choice but to arrest you."

Hap hinted at a smile, the aggression in his eyes giving way to amusement. "Well, then you best not come alone, Sheriff. It's going to take a lot more than just you to arrest me."

Dillon could still feel the lingering effects of Hap's vice-like fingers clamped around his forearm and knew the rancher was right.

CHAPTER 3

"I'm sorry, Sheriff. There won't be any delay of tomorrow's site visit. I've had it scheduled for three weeks."

Dillon sat behind his desk with the phone to his ear inside of the humble surroundings of the small Richland County Sheriff's Office. The building dated back to the 1940s and had seen little updating since then. It housed his office, two deputies, and seventy-three-year-old Adeline Rhodes who had worked as office secretary and dispatch for the sheriff's department for the last four decades. Adeline was as feisty as they came, her stout five-foot frame and still lightning-quick mind a match for any who walked through the office doors.

Dillon tried once again to plead his case to the Bureau of Land Management bureaucrat who was so intent on walking the Wilkes ranch. "I understand the inconvenience, Mr. Tuttle, but we're talking about an old man very set in his ways who also likely has access to firearms. I'm just asking for a few more days, maybe a week, to prepare him for your visit."

Bill Tuttle paused several seconds before responding, his voice dripping with the kind of condescending tone somehow so familiar to nearly every federal government employee Dillon Potts had had the misfortune of having to deal with. "Sheriff Potts, you are the sheriff of Richland County, correct?"

"Yes, Mr. Tuttle, I am."

This was followed by an even longer pause. "Well then, Sheriff, I suggest you do your job and let me do mine. I will be at that property tomorrow first thing in the morning and I expect you to keep myself and my team safe during our time there. We shouldn't be any more than a few hours. If you don't think yourself up to the task, I can always make a call into the State Patrol or have a few armed rangers drive on over from Yellowstone."

Dillon rolled his eyes, his fingers gripping the phone tighter as he fought the urge to fling it across the office. "That won't be necessary, Mr. Tuttle. I'll be there along with my deputy. You'll have your three hours. After this site visit what's your intention with those horses out there?"

Tuttle's tone immediately turned cheerful. "Well, if we find evidence of the spotted desert lizard on the property, we will have no choice but to take measures to protect their habitat as required by the Endangered Species Act. As you likely know we are the primary agency responsible for overseeing the protection of plant and wildlife listed as threatened or endangered."

Dillon closed his eyes, not wanting to hear the answer to his question, but knowing that answer was coming. "So, what happens to the horses?"

Tuttle didn't pause this time, seeming all too happy to let the sheriff know what he intended to do with the wild herd of horses. "We'll most likely have to terminate the herd. I don't have the budget to take on a relocation project. You ever try to catch a wild horse? It's not so easy and frankly having a frightened herd running around won't do the lizard habitat any favors."

"Just to be clear, you intend to kill an entire herd of horses to help out a lizard. Do I have that right?"

The happiness in Tuttle's voice became even more apparent. "Yes, that is what I intend to do. It's my job and it's what is best for both the endangered lizards *and* those horses. That can't be any kind of life for them, trying to find enough food to survive, the cold winters, the hot summers. As odd as it might seem right now, I assure you that this is a far more humane and logical solution."

"You aren't from Montana are you, Mr. Tuttle?"

The pause returned, as did the contemptuous tone. "Not that it matters, Sheriff, but no, I am *not* from Montana. I come from Chicago and graduated from Illinois State University with a degree in environmental studies."

"Sir, around here folks have a certain affinity for horses that goes back generations. Word will get out regarding what you intend to do and then you'll most likely find yourself with more than just one old rancher to have to contend with."

"Tomorrow morning, Sheriff, you be there with your deputy and do your damn job so me and my staff can do ours. I'm not too worried about a handful of disgruntled redneck ranchers. Goodbye."

The hand Dillon used to hold the phone was trembling, so furious was the sheriff over the government agent calling his neighbors, his family and his friends, disgruntled redneck ranchers. He slammed the phone down and took a slow, deep breath, then looked up to see the hard-blue eyes of Adeline Rhodes staring back at him.

"Feds still going out to the Wilkes ranch tomorrow?"

The sheriff nodded. He felt a headache looming.

"Yeah, and if they find some lizard out there, they plan to kill that herd of horses."

Adeline's eyes widened as her lips pursed. "What do you mean they're going to kill those horses? They can't do that! They can't just go onto a man's property and kill a bunch of animals in cold blood."

Dillon's headache arrived. "The man from the BLM seems to think so."

Adeline was having none of it, her right pointer finger jabbing in the air at the sheriff. "Now hold on there, Sheriff. This is *our* county. This is *your* county. People voted you into this office to protect them, not let some guy behind a federal government desk start shooting up a herd of horses that have been running that land long before you or I were born. And what about poor Hap? He *loves* those animals. They're pretty much all he's got left in this life. They kill those horses they might as well put a gun to his head as well and be done with it. You know I'm right. Don't sit there and say I'm not."

Dillon folded his hands atop his desk and looked back at his longtime secretary and sighed. "I know, Adeline. Believe me, I know. Now could you please shut the door and give me some peace? I got one crappy day coming up tomorrow. And tell Bobby I need him to meet me here in the office tomorrow morning."

Adeline shook her head and then pointed at Dillon again. "This is *your* county, Sheriff, not theirs. Don't you ever forget that."

After his office door closed the sheriff's gaze settled on the picture on his desk of his wife and two daughters getting into a small power boat where Dillon's father Stan was seated at the controls. Dillon remembered how wide his grin was as he took the photo. They had all gone fishing together that morning on a lake just outside of Shelby. It had been a beautiful day, one of those moments you don't fully appreciate at the time but then look back and wish you could return to over and over again. A month after the picture was taken Stan was in the hospital with a broken hip, an injury from which he had yet to recover from.

The man Dillon had long seen as indestructible was now just a tired shell of his former self. Stan Potts stayed in bed day after day, picking at tasteless food, staring at whatever images flashed across the TV screen, seemingly doing nothing more than waiting to die.

Dillon already figured that most people old enough to remember his dad still viewed him as a lesser sheriff than his father had been, and they were probably right. Stan Potts wouldn't have let some government bureaucrat dictate terms to him like he was an errand boy, especially not when it came to possibly harming the people of Richland County.

Tomorrow morning a group of federal agents had no intention of letting Hap Wilkes be. It already seemed clear they planned to kill the wild horses. Adeline was right. Those agents might as well just go on and kill Hap quick while they were at it. There was likely nothing in this world keeping the old rancher around but that herd and if he were to see them slaughtered on his own land that would be something too much for even a man as tough as Hap Wilkes to recover from.

CHAPTER 4

Connor didn't cry when his grandmother Shirley died. He didn't cry during the brief memorial service, or even when they handed him and his sister the urn with her ashes.

The tears finally came, though, when he read her letter. He cried the first time he read it and then the second and the third. Each time he felt the sadness, the hurt, and the confusion over those words written by the hand of a dying woman who had kept a secret for so long.

Connor's sister Sarah was just the opposite. She had cried terribly during their grandmother's final hours. Hospice had warned them it would take longer than they thought, and they were proven right. Grandma Shirley was ready to go but her body refused to leave just yet, as her breathing became slower, more labored, a terrible rasp filling the bedroom of the small home Connor and Sarah had shared with Grandma Shirley and Russ since the siblings' parents both died in a car accident three years earlier.

Sarah didn't cry over the letter, though. Instead, she seemed to grow stronger, more resilient from it, as if the letter answered a suspicion Sarah had held within herself for some time.

"Why didn't she let Dad know?"

Connor had repeated that question over and over. He repeated it to Sarah, and to Russ, the man who had been their grandmother's companion for the last twenty years. Russ was a quiet sort, well-intentioned, but his time with Grandma Shirley always felt more like friends rather than lovers—two people who both dragged more than a bit of regret and pain behind them and took comfort in helping one another get through the daily grind of simply being alive.

"Your grandma was a mystery, Connor. She kept a lot to herself and I never wanted to push her to share more than she wanted."

Connor looked away from Russ, the sound of the man's soft voice annoying him. The eighteen-year-old felt guilty for feeling that annoyance. Russ was in pain over Shirley's death just as he was, and Russ's own health was in decline as well. It wasn't so long ago that it was Grandma Shirley preparing herself for when Russ wouldn't be around. Then came her cancer and the terrible and debilitating treatments, until finally Connor and Sarah's grandmother decided no more. She was determined to live out her final weeks without the haze of the chemo that was killing her every bit as much as the tumors were.

Russ put his hand on Connor's shoulder, squeezed it gently, and then left the room. His walk was more of a slow shuffle. Although Russ had turned sixty just last year, he still had a full head of dark hair and a face that remained mostly free of lines. It was within Russ's eyes where his deep fatigue betrayed him. His body hurt far more than he let on, the autoimmune disease he had fought against for so many years was slowly getting the upper hand.

Sarah still held Grandma Shirley's letter. Two years younger than her brother, Sarah was finally, after the all too common plague of teenage awkwardness and uncertainty, transforming into the woman she would soon become. This newfound confidence, combined with her natural beauty, had not been lost on the boys of her school, much to her older brother's consternation.

Sarah had reached a height of five-foot-four, blessed with a lean womanly shape, and long brown hair with streaks of auburn, similar to that of her mother Jessica. Growing up, Jessica had often clashed with her daughter, but in the months before the car accident the two had begun to form a very close and understanding bond that those who are not mothers of daughters can never really understand.

At eighteen, Connor Beland was a broad-shouldered young man of six-feet, hungry for the opportunities of college and to be finally living life on his own. He had a round, friendly face, topped with blonde brown hair that he kept short. Despite being much larger and stronger than his sister, Connor had always deferred to her moods, wanting to avoid conflict whenever possible. It was a trait that had sometimes infuriated Connor's dad, Dex, who would tell his son not to let his sister or anyone else push him around.

Connor would listen to the advice with a barely concealed smirk, realizing the contradiction of being told not to let anyone push him around by a man who was constantly doing that very thing to him.

Like Sarah with her mom, Connor and his dad went through the same push and pull so common to fathers and sons. Where Jessica Beland was almost always warm and supportive, Dex Beland's moods alternated between approving and all-out condemnation. He gave his children love but if he thought them to be doing wrong, he was more than capable of giving them hell as well. In the Beland home, the worst crime Connor or Sarah could commit was disrespecting their mother.

On one such occasion, after saying something snide to his mom, Dex Beland grabbed his son and pushed him down, jabbing a finger into the teenage boy's chest and telling him to never talk to his mother like that again. When his dad turned to leave his room, Connor sat up and screamed out how he wished his father would just die. As soon as the words were spoken, Connor regretted them, while also fearing his dad would, for the first time, strike him with a closed fist.

Instead, Dex Beland looked down at his son and simply shook his head while whispering, "That'll happen soon enough." Jessica, as she so often did, played peacekeeper between father and child, eventually getting apologies out of both of them to each other.

Connor knew he couldn't be the only angry child to have ever spoken such a thing, just as his father couldn't have possibly known how terribly accurate and tragic his response to those words would prove to be.

The car accident happened three weeks later.

"It's a love story, Connor. Like Shakespeare, a tragic love story."

Connor turned to his sister, knowing his confusion was easily apparent on his face. "No, it's not. It's a lie. Why would Grandma not tell Dad the truth? She kept it from him, from us. It just seems so weird. It's like she was this whole other person none of us even knew about."

Connor had managed to annoy his sister yet again. "Who are you to judge her? You don't know what it was like, what she was going through. I'm not saying it was right what she did, but I'm also not going to condemn her for it. Grow up, Connor. Stop being such a judgmental jerk. Grandma just died."

"I'm not condemning anyone, Sarah. It just doesn't seem fair to Dad. She didn't tell him, but she goes and tells *us* after she's dead? Why?"

Sarah organized the sheets of yellow legal paper upon which Grandma Shirley had written her long letter of goodbye and subsequent confession, and then looked back at her brother. "Because she wanted to give you and me the opportunity she never gave Dad. Grandma said she thinks he's still alive. We should go see him. Let him know about Dad, and Mom . . . and us."

Connor was horrified by the thought as he wiped away another tear. "No way. Let it go. Grandma is dead. I'm graduating in a month and then I'm off to college. You have work and cheer camp coming up. We shouldn't leave Russ here alone. He might need us."

Both Connor and Sarah turned at the sound of a clearing throat. Russ stood in the doorway of the bedroom that Grandma Shirley had so recently passed away in.

"I'll be fine," he said. "If your Grandma Shirley mentioned something in her note to you, something you think she wanted you to do, don't worry about me. If you have to take a trip and you need some money to do it, I'll be happy to help."

Sarah's face broke into a wide smile. "Thanks, Russ. I really mean it."

Connor shook his head. "No, Sarah. We can't—"

Sarah cut her brother off as she gently placed their grandmother's handwritten letter onto his lap. "You read this again, Connor. This time try to put yourself in Grandma Shirley's place. What do you think Dad would want us to do? Or Mom?

Remember how Mom would tell Dad how he needed to stop bottling so many things up? That one day it was going to pour out of him all at once. You're just like Dad. You keep way too much bottled up while thinking that all those feelings will eventually just go away. They don't go away, Connor."

Both brother and sister were crying.

'Read the letter," Sarah said. "Read it one more time and then whatever you decide I'll support the decision."

Connor looked down at the pile of yellow paper in his hands, closed his eyes, and nodded. "Okay, Sarah. I'll read it."

CHAPTER 5

Dearest Connor and Sarah,

Well, it seems your old grandma is at the end of her journey. The doctors say it might be a matter of days or a few more weeks. I don't want you to be sad for my being gone, but rather, remember the good times we've had. Having you both here with me these last few years has been some of the most special and enjoyable years of my life.

Russ will be here to help you if you need it although with how strong the both of you have grown up to be, I think he might just need you more than you'll need him.

My eyes grow tired quickly these days so I should probably get to it.

First, I want you to know how much your parents loved you. Your dad was a complicated kind of man at times and was blessed to have the company of your mom, a very beautiful, patient, and understanding woman. The two of them created the both of you and that has been the greatest gift my son could ever have given me.

I wonder, though, if I deserved that gift. You see, there's something I've kept secret for a very long time. I was prepared to tell Dex about it but then the car accident happened, and that chance was gone. I knew then I should have had a talk with him much sooner but life kind of has a way of laughing at one's plans.

Anyways, I thought to just put the secret away again and not say anything to anyone because with your dad gone it just didn't seem like something that needed to be done. Do you remember that night last year when you were asking about my family, Sarah? I told you a bit about my own mother, a woman who just didn't seem capable of love. And then I spoke about the family friends I grew up with as a teenager after running away but didn't say too much more after that.

During that conversation I wanted so badly to blurt out what I'm about to share with you both now. I wanted to, but once again, as I have always done before, I lost the courage. You see, for as tough and determined I often appear to others your Grandma Shirley has always been a coward. I've always had a habit of running away from pain, and pain makes up so much of this secret.

I married at a young age, just 18 and right out of school. He was a man who allowed me the ability to finally get away from my mother, though, in reality he was nothing more than a different version of the same emotional prison. His name was Lyn Beland and he was a travelling salesman. He would be gone for weeks, even months at a time, leaving me to fend for myself until he eventually returned to town to party for a weekend before taking off once again. The marriage went on like that for a few years but each year I found Lyn stopping in less and less until one time he said he wouldn't be back for six months. He wanted to chase an opportunity way down in Florida of all places. He promised to send money but never did. He promised to call but didn't do that either.

I was on my own, which frankly wasn't such a bad thing. While I was still legally married, I considered myself single again. I was bit older and thought perhaps also a little wiser, ready to take on the world under my own terms. It also meant I would have more time to pursue my love of horses, something I had picked up while staying summers at my grandmother's ranch in Montana. So, with those memories filling my mind and heart, I loaded up my barely-running 1960 Chevy Impala, the same one you two have seen covered up in the carport outside, and drove back to the one place that held the only truly good memories of my youth — Montana.

It only took a couple of days for me to find work at one of the many horse ranches where I kept busy cleaning out stalls and feeding and watering the horses. It was hard work but helped me to feel good about myself and soon the owners of the ranch, a sweet older couple named Bill and Vye, treated me like an old friend and I discovered something for the first time in a very long time—happiness.

I oversaw the care of twenty-four horses being boarded at the property and was grateful for every minute of it. Especially the days when I would take one of them out for some exercise, galloping across the open pastures of Bill and Vye's ranch and realizing under that incredibly beautiful Montana sky just how perfect God's creation really is.

Then came the auction that fall. It was there my life changed forever and when the events that would later bring both of you into this world, took place.

At that time there was a large horse auction in October at the Montana Richland County Fairgrounds in Sidney, which is just a half- hour drive from Savage. It was at that auction I saw Hap Wilkes for the first time.

He was selling several horses, same as Bill and Vye were doing for some of their boarding clients. Hap walked his first horse out into the middle of the arena as the auctioneer began taking bids and I felt my heart start to beat like a little kettle drum inside my chest. Until that day I'd always scoffed at the phrase "love at first sight" thinking it was just a silly thing you read about in books, or watched in movies, and not something that actually happened in real life.

Well, for me, love at first sight happened as soon as I saw Hap. He was wearing the faded blue jeans I would later always find on him and the scuffed cowboy boots that adorned his feet regardless of the season. On that day he also had on a simple dark-blue western dress shirt and his beloved cowboy hat that he would later tell me belonged to the same grandfather who had first purchased what became known as the Wilkes ranch.

Even from a distance I could see and feel Hap's quiet confidence in the way he firmly yet gently handled the horse, and how he seemed to look out at the people while also looking right past them. He moved with a slow but deliberate athleticism, his lean frame hinting at the great strength I would later come to know.

For me, it was like looking at something for the very first time in my life—a real man.

Vye must have noticed my focus on every movement Hap made as she leaned down and pointed at him. "That's Hap Wilkes. His family's been around here even longer than Bill and I have. Might just be the best horse trainer in the state. People come from all around if they need a horse broken by him. When you buy a Wilkes horse you know you're buying quality."

I asked if I could meet him. Vye said sure and an hour later, standing near the side of his horse trailer, I said my first words to him.

"Hello, Mr. Wilkes. My name is Shirley. I just wanted to let you know you have some of the most beautiful, well-trained horses I've ever seen."

Hap glanced at me and mumbled a thank you and then went back to loading up his trailer. A lot of women would have considered that rude but it made Hap that much more interesting and I was more determined than ever to find out more about him.

"I would love to come by your ranch and look at any others you might be willing to sell."

Hap slammed one of the trailer's storage bins shut and looked me up and down and then looked over at Vye and Bill who were standing behind me. Bill, who was just the kindest man you'd ever meet, cleared his throat and spoke up.

"Mr. Wilkes, this is Shirley Beland. She's been working for us for some time now and is about the best ranch hand we've ever had. I'm happy to vouch for her character."

Finally, I had Hap's attention as his hazel-green eyes settled on me fully. I was determined not to be intimidated. Those eyes were so beautiful. Despite the ferocity of his stare there was a kindness in them as well and more than a hint of sadness. Though his face and body were of a man in his 30s, those remarkable eyes reflected someone much older.

"You looking to buy a horse, huh?"

I tried not to sound nervous but knew I failed. "Yes, maybe. I'd love to come take a look."

Hap scowled. "I don't do maybe, young lady. A horse isn't some plaything you take on as a maybe. It's either yes or it's no. So, what it is it?"

At this point I became a little angry. I didn't like anyone questioning my love or knowledge of horses, not even a man as sexy and powerful as Hap Wilkes. I straightened up and tried to fire it right back at him.

"It's a yes, Mr. Wilkes."

I was out at the Wilkes ranch the very next morning. He showed me three horses and then surprisingly offered me breakfast. I remember wondering why there wasn't a wife around but didn't get up the courage to ask him until later in the day.

I could tell he didn't like the question, but then, for whatever reason, Hap let down his guard just a bit and shared just a little of himself with a woman he had just met. His doing so let me know just how unhappy and desperate he really was for real companionship. He had been married for several years to a woman named January whose family had never approved of their daughter being the wife of a rancher. Her people were from Helena. Her father was a state senator and her mother the daughter of a banker.

As a younger woman January had apparently relished the idea of rebelling against her family's upper-class ideals and Hap was the perfect tool for her to do so. They had met at a rodeo that her mother's family was sponsoring, and Hap, then just out of high school, was trying his hand at bronco riding. She looked him up and weeks later they ran off and were married, much to the horror of both their families.

Soon after, she was living with Hap on his family's ranch and hating every second of it. Hap said January became angrier toward him with each passing season, more abusive, colder, their marriage nothing more than the sheet of paper representing the foolishness of youth. She had left Hap a year earlier, moving back to Helena under the guise of helping her mother care for her father who had suffered a stroke and was almost completely paralyzed.

Since that time, Hap was alone at his ranch. Both of his parents had already passed away and his only surviving sibling, a sister named Julia, was married and living out of state in Wyoming. It was a story so very similar to my own. Two people sharing the experience of a loveless first marriage that had left the both of us on our own.

By the end of that day I knew Hap was as attracted to me as I was to him, but he continued to keep both an emotional and physical distance between us. I told him I liked all three of the horses he showed me and then inquired if he needed help around the ranch. I said I could use the money and would be willing to work weekends while keeping my job at Bill and Vye's ranch as well.

I was surprised at how quickly Hap said yes.

And that, as they say, was that. I worked alongside Hap for the next three months, arriving every Saturday and Sunday morning and leaving late in the afternoon, my fascination for the man that he was growing with every visit. Hap continued to keep the relationship friendly but professional. Despite his wife's leaving, and being a Catholic, (I was raised and educated Catholic but had left the church behind as soon as I was able) he considered himself a still-married man and viewed me as a still-married woman.

We were falling deeply in love, though, and we both knew it.

31

Our first kiss happened while on an early-afternoon trail ride up to a place Hap called Vaughn's Hill, named after his grandfather. Hap enjoyed sharing his family's history and their connection to Ireland where many cousins, nieces and nephews still resided. Hap said Vaughn's Hill was his favorite place in the world, a place from where he could see the entire ranch, and if they were around, watch the wild horses that often made the property their home throughout the year. The horses were there that day, a hundred yards below us drinking from a stream that made its way toward the Yellowstone River. They looked so majestic, so powerful and free! I remember it being a cool winter afternoon with a clear sky and a slight breeze moving across the grass at our feet. Hap and I stood silently watching the horse herd for several minutes until I sensed Hap leaning over toward me. Suddenly, he kissed me lightly on the lips. Now I know you two might not be able to imagine your grandma as a young, and might I say, pretty darn attractive woman, but I was, and that first kiss from Hap was about the most pleasant thing to happen to me in quite some time.

I could tell he was worried he had crossed a line but before he had time to utter an apology, I pulled his head down toward mine and kissed him right back. You see, I wasn't interested in an apology for something I had wanted him to do since the very moment I first saw him. I just wanted more kissing.

We didn't say anything to each other all the way back to the house, but after the horses were put away Hap looked down at me and whispered his invitation in that low, growly voice of his. "Wanna stay for dinner?"

I stayed of course, not only for dinner, but breakfast the next morning. (Don't worry, your grandma won't go into any details of what happened during the time in between those two meals. Some things are better left unsaid.)

In fact, I stayed at Hap's ranch for nearly a year after that. We became friends and lovers, and together, made each other happier than we had ever thought possible before. Looking back, as I sit here writing all of this down with a hand barely strong enough to hold the pen, I'm quite certain outside of being a mother and grandmother, that year was the happiest of my life.

Some of the locals whispered about how Hap, who was almost fifteen years older than me, was having an affair with another woman while his wife was away. Bill and Vye never said anything negative about it even though I sensed they were concerned I would end up getting hurt. As for me, I didn't care about any of it. I only cared about waking up each day with Hap and sharing the work of running the ranch with him. He took to calling me Shirl, and I would call him Happy, because he seemed to be smiling more and more, the previous shell he had built around himself having cracked away during the time we spent together.

And then, one early morning, the phone rang. Hap rose from bed and walked into the kitchen to answer it. I could hear his voice, noting how it sounded different, less assured, almost weak, which was never a word I would have associated with Hap Wilkes.

When he came back into the bedroom, he told me January's father had died and that he was expected to make the drive over to Helena for the funeral. We both knew what that meant. He would arrive in Helena as January's husband and might very well leave there with the same designation, meaning our time together was coming to an end.

I'd like to say I handled that possibility better, but I didn't. I was angry and said things to Hap I have wished ever since I could take back. As for him, he said very little beyond it was his duty to be at the funeral and his duty to listen to what January had to say regarding their future as husband and wife.

I hated him for it. I really-really did. I cried, pleaded and begged, but Hap was determined to "do his duty" as he called it and make the trip to Helena. He told me to go back to Bill and Vye's and wait for him. So, that's what I did. I waited a week and then another and then on the third week I made the drive over to Hap's ranch.

January was there, coming out of the house and staring back at me as I got out of the car. She told me Hap wasn't there, that she had already heard all about me, and that I was no more than a silly distraction and no longer welcome in her home. She looked at me as if I was a child, her lean face hard, her eyes condemning me for the time I had spent with the husband she had long abandoned.

Then I saw Hap coming from the barn and for an all-too-brief moment, saw the joy in his eyes as he saw me too. Then those eyes went blank and the wall I thought removed from around him for good fell back into place.

January held out her hand to him like he was a pet. I watched in disappointed shock as Hap took his place beside her, his eyes avoiding mine. She told me they had worked things out and that I was to never step foot on the property again. I waited for Hap to say something, but he just stood there like a mute while looking at the ground at his feet. Finally, I heard something of the Hap I knew in the strong voice I had come to cherish.

"Give us a minute alone, January."

She protested but Hap's eyes simmered a warning that he would not be denied the request. January gave me one final, disgusted look and then made her way back into the house while Hap walked up to me and gently took my hands into his.

"I'm so sorry, Shirley but I made a promise. I made a sacred vow and I've always lived my life as a man of my word. For better or worse it's what it is. You're young. You have your whole life in front of you. Live it, enjoy it, and forget about this place. Forget about me. You'll be better off anyways."

My goodness did I cry so much right then. Hap held me as I sobbed and I sensed he might have been near to tears as well but when he pushed me from him to look down at me, his eyes were dry and he had returned to the unsmiling, emotionally distant version of himself I had first met months earlier.

"You have to go now."

Those were the last words Hap Wilkes ever said to me and I said nothing back. I just stood there for a moment longer, tears still streaming down my face as I watched Hap walk slowly back into the house that we had so recently shared with so much love and joy. I waited for him to turn around and look at me, but he never did. He simply walked through the door and closed it, and me, behind him.

I didn't stick around to fight for Hap. His turning away was too painful and that pain led me to leave Montana and head south to Arizona, hoping the distance between us would help to lessen the sense of loss and terrible disappointment.

It was two months later when the doctor informed me that I was nearly three months pregnant. I was carrying Hap's child, your father, inside of me. I had never felt so alone, so hopeless, so afraid, in all my life.

My husband Lyn somehow managed to track me down, calling me from Florida. He pretended to ask me how I was doing, but what he really wanted to know was if I had any money that I could send him. When I said I had none and I was pregnant with another man's child, he laughed and said he couldn't really blame me for it. When I asked for a divorce, he said sure, but then brought up something that gave me the first of many worries for how the world would view your father.

"Are you gonna make him a bastard? Feel free to give him my last name Beland if you want. It ain't worth much but at least he can think he wasn't just an afterthought following some fling you had. No sense him growing up thinking his mom was a whore."

Lyn didn't mean for his words to hurt so much. He was just too stupid to fully comprehend them. That said, I considered the possible wisdom of what he offered—a last name that would be easily explained to Dex and a life of growing up thinking he was the product of divorce instead of the byproduct of an affair.

It was a stupid thing of course. I know that now, and I'm pretty certain your dad always suspected there was much more to his story than I had been willing to share. Whatever thoughts he had on the subject he kept to himself for the most part, though, and we went on getting by, just the two of us against the world.

Though I never spoke to Hap again I did see him one more time. It was right after your dad's high school graduation. I met Dex in the parking lot of the school, surrounded by his classmates and their families, and gave him a hug. He had grown into a younger version of the man you both came to know as your dad. Tall, lean, and like Hap, he had an easy, relaxed athleticism to him, and those same big hazel-green eyes. The resemblance, in fact, had become rather remarkable and caused me more than a little pained regret when I would look at Dex and then be reminded of the time I had with Hap.

Anyways, I caught a familiar face out of the corner of my eye as I made my way back to my car. Not actually a face but an all too familiar, tattered cowboy hat. There was Hap, looking older, more worn, even a touch haggard, but it was still him. I have to assume he had been keeping track of me from time to time, the same as I had done to him, and suspected Dex could be his son. I don't think he saw me. His eyes were focused on Dex, watching as your dad moved through the large crowd of people, stopping regularly to shake hands with a teacher, or have his picture taken with a friend, until finally he found your mom and they began walking arm in arm to the little black Mustang Jessica had back then. The two of them started dating during Jessica's senior year when Dex was a junior and now after his own graduation from high school, Dex planned on following Jessica to the same college she was already attending where they could continue their relationship.

Hap was staring intently at the two of them and though I'm not positive, I think he had a little smile on his face. Then the moment passed as several vehicles moved in front of me. When I could once again look across the parking lot, the man I thought was Hap was no longer there.

Again, as I had done so many times before, I told myself to let Dex know the truth. Each time I lost my courage and resigned myself to do it next year, and then the year after. Soon, your mother and father were married, became parents, and the telling of that truth seemed to become less important as their lives were filled with their own family and creating their own history.

That was the convenient excuse I had created of course. I know that now. Like I said, I was a terrible coward wanting to avoid painful memories by burying them deep down where even I might someday forget them.

Try as I might, I could never forget Hap Wilkes. He was, and will always be, my one true love in this life.

So, here I am, with time running away even more quickly from me, and finally after all of these years telling you two the truth of at least part of who your dad really was. One of my greatest regrets, one that I am now forced to take with me to the very end, is not telling Dex before the accident.

I can never forgive myself for that.

What I can do, though, is give you two the opportunity I never gave your dad. The last time I checked, Hap Wilkes is still alive. He has to be nearly eighty by now but as tough as he was, he might just go another eighty before he's done. If you want, take my old Impala up to Savage, Montana. You'll find Hap there likely still living in the very same house we shared together forty years ago.

If you do make the trip don't let him spook you. Hap takes a while to warm to newcomers. He likes to size people up, just like Dex used to do. Get past that and you might find the same kind and caring man I did. Tell him about yourselves, about your mom, and about his son.

It's up to you. Whether you make the trip or not doesn't matter much to me because I'll be long gone by then. Who knows, though? Maybe someway, somehow, I can be watching over you. I'd love to see Hap's face when you drive up in my old car!

I am so proud of the both of you. Please don't ever waste the time you are given because you can't ever get it back.

Love forever,
Grandma S.

CHAPTER 6

"Bright and early, just like you asked, Sheriff."

Dillon looked up to see thirty-four-year-old Bobby Houston standing in the doorway of his office. The deputy's massive shoulders nearly touched each side of the door frame.

Bobby had been a star linebacker for Montana State University before a knee injury cut short his dreams of playing pro. Two years after Houston graduated college with a criminal justice degree the sheriff hired him on as his deputy and since that time Deputy Houston had garnered the respect of both his sheriff and the citizens of Richland County.

At six-foot-four, and two-hundred-and-fifty pounds, Bobby Houston was an imposing physical presence, but on the job, he rarely used his size and strength to obtain results. Far more valuable was his patience and understanding. He was a man known for listening first and always trying to resolve disputes by mutual agreement.

"So, we're heading out to the Wilkes place, huh? Never been out that way but I've been told old Hap Wilkes isn't one for visitors. I've only seen him in church, always coming in late and then leaving early."

The sheriff stood up from his desk and grabbed his hat while nodding back at his deputy. "Yeah, he's pretty much the personification of a grumpy old man. That doesn't mean what those morons from the Bureau of Land Management are thinking of doing is right, though."

Deputy Houston grunted as he shook his head. "Never much cared for big government. Rather they just left us alone to take care of our own business. Am I right?"

The sheriff looked over and saw Bobby's oversized black fist extended toward him, awaiting the cursory fist-bump. "Yeah, you got that right, Bobby. I need you ready to help keep Mr. Wilkes from going off. He's got a short fuse and is rightfully upset at these feds coming in crawling all over his property. I don't want him getting himself so worked up he drops dead on us, hurts himself, or tries to hurt someone else."

Bobby's eyes narrowed. "The guy is like eighty, right? How much of a threat could he really be?"

The sheriff gave Deputy Houston a look that made clear his instructions were not to be taken lightly. "Hap Wilkes is old but he's also real old school, Bobby. There was a time when nobody, and I mean *nobody,* around here would think of messing with him, my dad included. So, when I say be ready you make darn sure you do just that. I don't want anyone getting hurt today."

The drive from the station to the Wilkes place took nearly twenty minutes. During that time the sheriff and his deputy said nothing. The absence of conversation allowed them to fully enjoy the simple pleasure of watching the early spring Montana landscape pass by. The sky was dotted with light, quickly moving clouds. A light breeze pushed the tall grasses of the fields and rolling hills back and forth, reminding the sheriff of some great mass of uncombed, always-moving hair that sat atop the head of the earth.

The tranquility was broken by the flashing lights of two white Bureau of Land Management SUVs parked on the side of the road directly opposite the entrance to the ranch.

"Ah, shoot," Sheriff Potts mumbled. He had wanted to be the first out to Hap's property. He spied the bald head of the man he knew had to be Tuttle moving from behind one of the two SUVs. Four other armed BLM representatives were with him.

"They show up here with assault rifles?" The surprise in Deputy Houston's voice mirrored what the sheriff was already thinking.

"Looks that way."

As the sheriff pulled his vehicle to the side of the road, he looked over to see Tuttle's mocking smile spreading across his fleshy face. Deputy Houston noticed Tuttle as well and grunted his disapproval.

"Never met the guy but that little fella right there looks like a total tool."

The sheriff didn't respond to his deputy's observation of Bill Tuttle, having already opened the door to make his way outside.

"Well hello there, Sheriff. It's nice to meet you in person. I hope you don't mind my bringing along a few others from my department but based on your warnings of how unstable Mr. Wilkes is I thought it prudent. Not that I don't think you're up to the task of course. It's just that I've always been a more safe than sorry kind of guy."

The sheriff was pissed and didn't bother trying to hide it. He walked quickly across the narrow county road to confront the BLM supervisor. "You bring armed men into my county you darn well better let me know ahead of time, Mr. Tuttle. This is a serious breach of protocol and professional courtesy and as you can likely already see, I'm none too happy about it. Tell your men to put

43

those rifles away. You confront Mr. Wilkes with those things and he's likely to come out shooting."

The much shorter Tuttle lifted his chin defiantly in response to the sheriff's anger. "I am an officer of the federal government, Sheriff. I don't answer to you. I also assumed safety was first and foremost. Was I wrong to think so?"

The sheriff took another step toward Tuttle, glaring down at the smaller man who suddenly no longer looked nearly so confident. "If you're really worried about safety, Mr. Tuttle, you'll keep those assault rifles out of my sight, understand? Leave them in your vehicles. I'll make my way down to the house and let Mr. Wilkes know that you're coming in to walk his property and then once you're done doing that, you're going to get the hell out of here."

The government bureaucrat's face tightened as he held the sheriff's gaze for a few seconds before lowering his head and waving his hand in a downward motion to the armed BLM officers. "Leave the weapons in the truck unless I order otherwise." Tuttle turned back to face Sheriff Potts. "There you go, Sheriff. Just like you asked. Now, if you don't mind, I want to introduce you to Professor Joyce Hammond. She will be the primary consultant on our study of the Wilkes property and the one whose report will be used to determine the need for further action."

The person Sheriff Potts had mistakenly assumed was another man was in fact a tall, very thin, middle-aged woman. She had gray-streaked, shoulder-length hair tied back into a ponytail, a long, lean face devoid of any make-up, and large, brown eyes that appeared both intelligent and kind.

Professor Hammond offered her hand to the sheriff. He shook it briefly as she introduced herself. "It's a pleasure to meet you, Sheriff. I'm sorry for the fuss but we have a job to do. I assure you I'll be as quick as possible during the on-site visit."

The sheriff glanced down at Tuttle and then nodded briefly at Professor Hammond. "Seems like a lot of fuss for some lizard, Professor. Is this really worth turning an old man's life upside down?"

Joyce withdrew her hand as the kindness in her eyes quickly vacated.

"That lizard is a protected species. It's our duty to follow the law which is something I assume you would like to do as well."

The sheriff grimaced as he noticed the smirk return to Tuttle's face. "That's why I'm here, Professor. To make sure everyone follows the law. So, how about we get this dog and pony show—"

Deputy Houston's voice cut off Dillon's remarks. "I think we might have a situation, Sheriff."

Some three hundred yards away was the bent and struggling form of Hap Wilkes shuffling slowly down his long driveway toward where Sheriff Potts and the others were gathered. Hap's left leg dragged behind him, leaving a long, shallow trail in the dirt where the tip of his cowboy boot cut into the ground.

Cradled in the rancher's arms was a shotgun.

CHAPTER 7

"She's beautiful!"

Sarah smiled at her brother's enthusiasm while they both looked at their Grandma Shirley's 1960 Chevy Impala that Russ had just removed the cover from. Though the once-gleaming light blue paint was now heavily faded and in many places marked with rust, especially over its flat hardtop roof, the great mass of steel and chrome still managed a powerful aura of dignity that represented a long-ago era when "Built in America" had been the envy of the world.

Russ had both his hands resting on the hood of the car enjoying Connor's appreciation of the Impala but also seeming to withdraw into himself for a moment. The empty car was a reminder Shirley was truly gone. He turned to see Sarah looking through the passenger window, her eyes wide and excited at the journey that lay ahead and for a second, Russ saw Shirley there instead, healthy and strong, long before the cancer had slowly but steadily taken the life from her.

"I'm not much of a mechanic but I tinkered on her over the years, worked on the carb, replaced some fuel lines, flushed the radiator out, new oil and filter, and topped off the gas with some stabilizer. That was nearly five years ago so no guarantees. I already put the charger on the battery. Let's see if she'll fire up for you two."

Connor moved to take a position behind the steering wheel, but Sarah was there first, sliding across the front seat and looking out through the dust-covered windshield, the smile on her face having grown even wider. Again, Russ experienced the bittersweet juxtaposition of Sarah as Shirley as he silently wished Shirley was here to see her two grandchildren preparing to drive away in her old car. He knew she would have gotten a kick out of it. Though she never came right out and said it, the Impala represented a time when Shirley felt the most free and alive. It's why she never sold it even as a few offers would trickle in over the years from hopeful buyers who saw the car parked outside their home.

"Can I turn the key?" Sarah asked.

Russ nodded. "Let her rip!"

The old Detroit-built V8 turned over slowly, groaning like some ancient beast awoken from a long slumber.

"Pump the pedal a few times while you turn the key."

Sarah followed Russ's instruction, ramming the gas to the floorboard in quick succession as the ignition was turned. This time the V8 sounded more enthusiastic but was still unwilling to come to life.

"That's it," Russ said. "Keep at it."

Connor stood next to Russ and noted the powerful smell of gas coming from the Impala's carburetor. "She's gonna flood it."

Russ ignored Connor's concern, quietly whispering to himself for the car to start. "C'mon, Shirley. Give us a sign. Tell me you're here."

The engine fired as a great cloud of dark smoke belched from the rear of the Impala right before it settled into a low gurgling idle. Sarah cried out triumphantly while Connor ran a hand lightly over the roof of the car, shaking his head slowly from side to side.

"I've never heard a car sound so awesome."

Russ looked over the dash gauges, saw the tank was reading full, the temperature was holding steady, and the battery was charging. The Impala, at least for now, was running perfectly.

Sarah reached down to turn the radio on and was delighted to hear the sound of music crackling from the speakers. The song was unknown to her, a number titled *Go Now* by the Moody Blues. Russ knew the song well. Shirley played it often while cleaning the house on Sundays, singing alone, lost in a memory from a time long before Russ was part of her life.

He never resented Shirley for her secrets, respecting that everyone holds things sacred only to them. It was part of what made her who she was, and Russ missed her terribly while at the same time being grateful for the time they shared. While those years were not marked by great romance there had always been undeniable friendship and caring and Russ knew that sadly, many go through life not knowing any of those things.

Sarah tilted her head upward and inhaled deeply and then looked outside the driver door window at Russ. "You smell that? It's like—"

Russ felt tears forming in his eyes as he interrupted Sarah. "It's like flowers. Your grandma's favorite fragrance was Chanel. She said she'd worn it since high school. That's what you smell. It's your Grandma Shirley."

Sarah went quiet as she gripped the Impala's massive steering wheel, the car's interior vibrating softly in rhythm to the engine as the Moody Blues song came to an end.

"So, you two are definitely doing this?" Russ asked. "You're going to make the trip up to Montana?"

49

Sarah said nothing while she nodded her head and then looked over at her brother. Connor paused and then seeing his sister once again struggling to keep her own tears at bay, shrugged his broad shoulders. "Yeah, we're going."

Russ stood up and offered a hint of a smile, his eyes still moist with emotion. "Okay, then there's something your grandma wanted you to take with you if you decided to go. Wait here."

Both Connor and Sarah watched as Russ walked into the house and then re-emerged a short time later carrying a single white envelope. He reached into the car and handed it to Sarah. "Shirley wanted you two to make up your own mind about the trip but told me if you *did* decide to make it, she hoped you'd be able to deliver this letter."

Sarah looked down at the sealed envelope where she found a single word scrawled on the front of it in her grandmother's handwriting:

Hap

"Do you know what it says?"

Russ shook his head and smiled. "No. Whatever she wrote is between Shirley and Hap and is none of my business. I would have delivered it for her if you two had decided not to drive up there yourself, but I know it would have meant so much to your grandma that you are the ones to give him that letter."

Sarah opened the Impala's cavernous glove box and gently placed the envelope inside. She then opened the driver's door and stepped out while leaving the car running, the tone of its idle seeming to hint at the big car's impatience to finally be on the road again.

"You two be careful," Russ said. "Call and let me know how you're doing."

Sarah hugged Russ tightly and then stood back as Connor shook his hand. "We will, Russ. I'll keep her out of trouble."

Sarah rolled her eyes as she moved to take her place back behind the wheel of the Impala. "Yeah right, nerd. Get in."

Russ stood behind the Impala and watched as Sarah put the car into gear and began slowly driving it across the yard and onto the road that would mark the beginning of the two siblings' journey to a place that was home to their grandmother's past.

The light scent of Chanel still lingered, and another song drifted out from behind the Impala's open windows—*To Sir with Love*.

That too was one of Shirley's favorites.

CHAPTER 8

Sheriff Potts moved quickly to try to diffuse what he knew could quickly escalate into a very dangerous situation.

"Your men are to keep those rifles in the vehicles, Mr. Tuttle."

Tuttle had already moved himself behind one of the SUVs, his eyes wide with fear.

"You don't order *me* sheriff and I assure you that we're ready to protect ourselves if you can't."

"Bobby," the sheriff said, "keep everyone behind the vehicles and as calm as possible. I'm going to go have a talk with Mr. Wilkes."

Deputy Houston looked out to where the rancher now stood just beyond the road from them.

"You sure that's a good idea? That old boy looks ready to go out in a blaze of glory right about now."

Sheriff Potts let out a quick sigh and nodded to his deputy. "Yeah, but Hap Wilkes isn't a killer. He's just ticked off and frankly I don't blame him."

The sheriff held his arms out to his sides and began moving slowly across the road. "I'm coming over to talk, Mr. Wilkes. Nobody here is looking for any trouble, but you raise up that shotgun and this situation goes bad real quick, understand?"

Hap lowered the weapon. "I'm just out for a walk, Sheriff. Nothing in the law says a man can't walk his own property, right? Or maybe those feds over there already consider this *their* land. If they do, then you're right—this thing goes bad quick."

Dillon continued making his way slowly and deliberately toward Hap. "This is a long walk out here, Mr. Wilkes. Why didn't you drive?"

Hap frowned and then shook his head. "Truck wouldn't start. Got some electrical thing. Battery's dead. Thing's been hassling me for the last month."

The sheriff looked around to see where Hap's dog was but couldn't locate it. "How about your dog?"

Hap chuckled. "Dog got in your head, did he? I left him back home keeping watch."

"Why not ride your horse out here?"

The rancher's eyes narrowed as he glared across the road at the collection of Bureau of Land Management SUVs. "Didn't want someone taking shots at her. Been hearing talk about how the government wants to get into the horse-killing business."

Dillon stood no more than ten feet from the rancher. Hap looked tired and disheveled. His face was speckled with stubble. The walk down the long drive had clearly taken a toll as his breath whistled between pursed lips.

"Mr. Wilkes," Dillon said. "These people are just doing a job. How about you and I wait inside your house, let them get to it, and then it'll all be over."

Hap dipped his head slightly to the right, his hard, sun-dried stare peeking out from just under the brim of his cowboy hat. "I thought I made it clear to you yesterday, Sheriff. I said to tell these feds they're not to come onto my land. That seems clear enough to me. So, why are they here? You taking their side in this? Is that what's going on?"

A warning siren sounded inside the sheriff's head as he realized how close Hap's rage was to turning into something deadly. "No. I'm doing my job the same as them."

Hap sneered at the young sheriff. "Don't go hiding behind that badge, Dillon. In this life you choose to do right, or you choose different. Stop talking and make that choice. Choose which side of this line you're to be standing on and then get the hell out of my way."

The sheriff's right hand instinctively moved toward his sidearm. "You know it's more complicated than that, Mr. Wilkes. I have an obligation to follow the law and the law says these feds have a right to do a site check of your property to determine if there's an endangered species on it. The sooner you let them do their job the sooner it'll be over."

Hap glanced down at the sheriff's creeping right hand. "You really think so, Sheriff? That after today this will be over? No, you lied to me right then and you know it. These feds, they'll keep coming and coming, taking and taking. It's what they do. It's what they *always* do, and I've had it. No more. Not this time. If they want to take from me, well, this time they are going to have to really *take* it because I won't just give it to them. They want to mess with that herd of horses that I know have been living just fine with all those little lizards out there, then they're going to have to mess with me first. Now you look, Sheriff. You look real good and know I'm not just talking. I'll take this thing all the way. You understand me?"

Hap's words hissed from between clenched teeth. "I said you look at me, Dillon Potts. Look at me and know I am serious business. Take those feds away from my home or there's going to be blood spilled. There's nothing left for me to lose in this life except my pride and my pride won't allow me to watch these people trample over *my* land and harm those horses."

Dillon sensed Hap struggling for breath and saw the lines of sweat dripping down his face. Hap's leathery skin, normally sun-darkened, now looked mottled and pale. A flash of panic fired out from the rancher's eyes as he suddenly dropped the shotgun. He took two halting steps to his right and then fell onto his knees as a low groan shook him.

The sheriff tried to move quickly enough to catch the old rancher, but he was too slow. The right side of Hap's face slammed into the hard-packed dirt where he remained unmoving but for the small cloud of dust gathering near his mouth where the sound of uneven, wheezing breath was the only indication that he was still alive.

"Bobby, get an ambulance out here. Now!"

Deputy Houston was already nearly to where the sheriff was moving Hap onto his back to check the rancher's vitals. A moment later and he was leaning down on the other side of Hap and looking at the sheriff.

"I called it in, Sheriff. Is it a heart attack?"

Dillon shrugged as he located a weak and erratic pulse. "Don't know. Could be another stroke."

Both law enforcement officers turned toward the sound of approaching footsteps. Tuttle glanced down at Hap. "Is the old guy going to be okay, Sheriff?" The question was devoid of even a hint of concern for Hap's well-being.

"Right now, it doesn't look too good, Mr. Tuttle. I'm going to ask that you please return to your vehicle."

A thin smile crept across the BLM supervisor's face. "It seems clear you have this situation under control, Sheriff. I'm going to go ahead and proceed with the site check. It doesn't appear Mr. Wilkes will be a threat to us at the moment so for the safety of all concerned this would be a good time to proceed with why we all came here today."

Deputy Houston rose up and moved himself directly in front of Tuttle, his large pointer finger slamming into the government bureaucrat's chest. "Like hell you are. The property owner is lying here dying and you want to go on like nothing happened? What is wrong with you, man?"

Tuttle took several steps back, clearly intimidated by Bobby's powerful build. "I suggest you get your deputy under control, Sheriff or I'll have your entire department investigated. I have contacts in the DOJ. I would also remind *you*, Deputy, that I didn't come here unarmed."

Bobby looked over toward the parked SUV's and spotted the armed BLM agents pointing their assault rifles back at him. His arm extended outward with incredible speed as he grabbed the front of Tuttle's dress shirt and yanking the much smaller man forward. The deputy's face loomed over Tuttle as he bellowed his dissatisfaction at anyone thinking they could point a weapon at him.

"I'm a deputy sheriff. You threaten me like that again and I'll arrest your worthless butt and throw you in a hole so deep nobody will find you."

Dillon grabbed onto Bobby's muscular arm. "That's enough," he said.

Bobby continued to hold tight to Tuttle.

"Deputy, that's an order. Let him go and step away."

Bobby released Tuttle and watched with satisfaction as he fell backwards onto the dirt.

Dillon moved to help Tuttle up. He understood Bobby's outrage, even shared much of it, but the sheriff also knew the legal obligations of his department required he make accommodations to the feds. He also knew Tuttle's threat of contacting the DOJ was likely not an empty one.

"I apologize for that, Mr. Tuttle. Seems we're all a bit on edge here."

Tuttle quickly recovered his composure, believing himself already safe from the deputy's threat. "Quite the department you run here, Sheriff. I expect to see a full review of this officer's behavior, understood?"

The sheriff nodded while clearing his throat. "Of course, Mr. Tuttle. I assure you this is normally not how we operate. I suggest at this point that you and your people go on ahead and do your site visit, take samples, whatever else it is you think needs to be done here, okay?"

Tuttle brushed the dust off his slacks and then huffed at the sheriff's offer. "We'll do that, Sheriff. Then you get me the incident report on you deputy's actions. If I see any evidence of favoritism, I assure you there will be a full federal investigation into this. That man clearly isn't worthy of the badge you put on him."

Dillon felt both his fists clench tightly as he fought back the urge to grab the BLM agent himself and finish what Bobby had started. "Thank you for the advice. Now, if you don't mind, I have a man in need of medical attention and you apparently have some lizards you need to look for."

The sheriff watched and listened as Tuttle barked orders for his team to drive onto the property.

"That is one nasty little son-of-a-bitch," Bobby seethed.

Dillon said nothing as he focused on monitoring Hap's pulse. The rancher was hanging on, but his heartbeat was becoming increasingly erratic.

In the distance the sound of an approaching ambulance could be heard as the sheriff silently repeated a phrase to himself that he had been saying more and more of late.

I hate this damn job.

CHAPTER 9

"It's 345 Everson Street—just a few miles more."

Sarah was looking down at the GPS app on her phone while her brother drove, having located the address of Julia Meyers-Wilkes, Hap's sister. It had taken Sarah and Connor nearly nine hours of driving from Arizona to reach the small town of Baggs, Wyoming. The Impala drove flawlessly, the low rumble of its V8 propelling itself down seemingly unending stretches of highway as they passed countless towns, cities, and open farmland.

"There's another one," Connor said. "That's the third church in the last mile. I think this place has more churches than people."

Connor's exaggeration was not all that far from the truth. Baggs, with a population of just over four-hundred, was noted for its abundance of churches, from the light blue, single-story Catholic Lady of the Sage structure off of Highway 70, to the LDS church they had just passed when nearing the turn onto Everson Street.

"There it is Connor—the double-wide."

345 Everson was an older mobile home with a yard that hinted at better days long since gone. The grass was nearly a foot high and almost entirely overtaken by various weeds. The blue paint of the home itself was faded and cracked or missing entirely.

A portion of the roof was missing as well, covered over by a tarp. The driveway was a mixture of weeds and dirt. It appeared no car had parked there in years.

"I think it's abandoned."

Sarah's heart sank, knowing her brother might be right. The place looked empty. "Wait, I think that's smoke coming out of the chimney."

Connor slowed down and moved the Impala to the side of the road, then looked at where his sister was pointing. It did look to be a faint wisp of smoke coming from the rusted-out metallic chimney pipe.

He glanced over at Sarah. "Well, what now?"

"Park in the driveway."

Connor knew if he had been by himself, he would never have tried to locate Hap's sister. Sarah was different, though. Once she had her mind made up to do something no amount of convincing her to do otherwise would change that determination. His sister was now obsessed with learning more about the grandfather they never knew before meeting him in person and this visit with Hap's sister was a way to do just that.

"C'mon Connor, park the car in the driveway. We can't leave it sitting here on the side of the road. Besides, I really have to pee."

Connor was about to pull into the driveway when he froze. The home's front door opened, and an old woman emerged onto the small, covered platform that marked the entrance. "You think that's her? Julia Wilkes?"

The woman was tiny, well under five-feet, her back bent with age, and a head covered in thinning, reddish-white hair. She wore a black dress that fell to her ankles, white slippers, and her fingers were curled inward with arthritis.

"She'd be about the right age," Sarah said.

The old woman was calling out for something. A moment later a large white cat bounded through the yard and up the three steps to the front door.

"There you are, Mr. Whiskers! There you are! Come in now! Right this way!"

"Great, we're related to a crazy cat lady."

Sarah punched her brother's shoulder.

"Shut up. I think she's cute."

Connor smiled, knowing he was getting on his sister's nerves, something he had always found easy to accomplish. "Cute? You mean the cat or the old woman?"

Sarah's eyes flashed genuine anger, very similar to the look the grandfather she had not yet met would get when his own temper began to burn hot. "Park the car."

Connor put the Impala into gear and drove it across the road and into the overgrown driveway and then shut it off. "Last chance to change your mind. You might not like what you find out about these people."

Sarah stared at the dilapidated double-wide and smiled. "I'm not going to hide from my past like Grandma Shirley. I want to know who I come from."

Soon brother and sister stood at the entrance to the mobile home waiting for someone to respond to their knock.

The door opened.

CHAPTER 10

For the second time in as many years, Hap Wilkes should have died.

Death actually visited him three times during the forty-mile ambulance ride from his ranch to the hospital in Culbertson. Each time, the medics managed to resuscitate, marveling how the old rancher clung so tenaciously to life.

By the time Hap was being wheeled into the emergency room the medics had ruled out a heart attack. Within thirty minutes it was suspected he was suffering from a pulmonary embolism, a serious clot within one or more of the major arteries in the lungs. A CT scan confirmed the diagnosis.

An aggressive round of anticoagulants was administered as the emergency room physicians waited to see if the rancher's condition would stabilize. When Hap's breathing worsened once again and his heart began beating rapidly as it fought against the lack of oxygen, the medical team injected thrombolytic, a powerful and somewhat dangerous clot-dissolving drug, directly into Hap's lungs, hoping to more quickly break up the clotting.

Within an hour after that injection Hap Wilkes was demanding he be allowed to go home. So furious did those demands come the staff feared he would complicate his recovery and so the rancher was sedated.

It was during the deep sleep following the sedation that Hap dreamed of Shirley, her familiar voice seeming to come from a vast distance away. The great pain, regret, and joy in hearing that voice again after so many years caused Hap's eyes to threaten tears while he lay unconscious in the Culbertson hospital bed.

God, he missed her.

Hello, Hap.

Shirley, I'm sorry. I'm sorry it's been so long. I'm sorry . . . hell, I'm sorry for everything. I tried. I really did, but she wouldn't allow it and I made a promise. It was a vow and you know—

Sshh. I don't need your apology, Hap. There's nothing to apologize for between us. Not anymore. Don't waste time with guilt. Life is too short for that and the last thing I want for you is wasting time on regret.

I should have tried harder back then. I was weak—stupid and weak.

Hap, I need you to listen. I have something to tell you and there's not much time.

I loved you, Shirley. I should have told you. I should have said it when I had the chance. All of this time wasted. Have you been happy? I was told you found someone. I hope he's been a good man to you. You deserve to be loved. You deserved so much better than what I wouldn't give. I know that now. I should have known it then.

Shirley stood directly in front of Hap, somehow looking as young, beautiful, and vibrant as when they spent that year together alone at the ranch—the best year of Hap's life. She couldn't possibly be this young anymore, though. And yet, somehow, she was.

Her medium-length dark hair sat high on her head in the fashion of all those years earlier, the hair's color complimenting the deep brown of her eyes. Her lean body was the result of a love of horses and a willingness to engage in hard work. Shirley was what many then called a natural beauty, an appearance free from pretense, equally at home atop a horse galloping through open fields or at the table of a fine dining establishment.

She did not smile easily, but when that smile revealed itself her features would soften, hinting at the deep vulnerability that housed itself just below the somewhat tougher, protective exterior. It was her vulnerability that made up so much of what attracted Hap to the younger woman. He wanted to protect her from the too often harsh realities of the world, only to discover what Shirley needed protecting from the most was him.

This isn't about what I deserved, Hap. It's not about us. It never should have been just about us. We were both too selfish, weren't we? Too proud, too afraid, and too weak.

Hap knew Shirley was right, wishing he had heard her say those words to him long ago. Maybe then it would have given him the courage to do what was right. Courage he had refused to find in himself.

My son—you're here to tell me about my son.

Shirley's eyes reflected great sadness. It was the unmistakable, unfathomable depth of pain that is a mother having lost a child. Hap knew of Shirley's loss, enough of it anyways. His sister had told him a few years earlier. Julia had always tried to remind her brother of his time with Shirley and the possible outcome of that relationship. It was an outcome Hap had long felt great shame in not confirming.

So, you did know about him? Our son?

Hap closed his eyes and nodded. *Julia told me you had a boy. She was always checking in on you, trying to keep me updated. She suspected he was mine, given the timing. I was trying my best to be a husband to January by then. We were already planning on adopting a child ourselves. I told Julia to stay out of it, that it wasn't any of her business. I just…I just left it alone, Shirley. You deserved happiness and I wasn't the one to give it to you. It wasn't right what I did. I know that but there's nothing to be done about it now. If I could change it, I'd like to think I would but any hope for that second chance died away like everything else.*

That's not true, Hap. There's someone coming to see you very soon. Give them the opportunity to know the man I once knew. Help them to learn who they are. If you ever really loved me, you'll do this last thing.

Shirley was turning away, leaving Hap to stand alone in the darkness of his own dream. It was a darkness that gripped the rancher with terror, its depth so absolute and unknowable.

Shirley! Please stay with me!

Hap immediately sensed the irony of his plea. Shirley had once cried out those very words to him long ago. He could no longer see her but sensed she was looking back at him from the great void, her voice circling his mind, comforting him, as it had done all those years earlier. Tears threatened. Hap loathed crying.

The tears came and wouldn't stop. Torrents of regret, shame, the seething resentment of time lost never to be returned, welled up from a place he had attempted to bury away from memory—a memory that left him standing in this terrible darkness, feeling so alone, so hopeless, so without the love he knew would have been.

I'll wait for you, Hap. To forever and back, I'll wait.

CHAPTER 11

"Hello? Can I help you?"

Julia Wilkes appeared like a wizened gnome as her large, expressive eyes looked up at the two young people standing at the entrance to her home. She didn't have lines on her lean face so much as deep crevices, making it impossible to guess how she may have appeared as a young woman.

Connor was the first to speak. "Uh, Ms. Wilkes, my name is Connor, and this is Sarah. We were told you know Hap Wilkes."

Julia's eyes darted from Connor and then to Sarah, her expression uncertain and guarded. "That's right. Hap is my brother. Is he okay?"

Sarah moved a half-step forward with a reassuring smile. "We think so, that is, we *hope* so. We come from Arizona and are on our way to see him at his ranch in Montana."

Julia's demeanor instantly transformed from uncertainty to the realization of who Connor and Sarah both were. "Are you related to Shirley?"

Sarah nodded her head with enthusiasm that matched that of Julia's. "That's right. Shirley was our grandmother. We've been living with her the last few years. She just recently passed away from cancer."

Julia's eyes conveyed both sadness and disappointment. "Oh, I am so sorry. How awful for you. I knew about your parents' passing not so long ago and now this. What a terrible thing. I apologize for my lack of manners. Please, come in!"

The interior of the double-wide was both much larger and cleaner than its outside appearance would indicate. The furnishings, though dated, were in good condition and the home smelled of freshly baked cookies.

"I don't get many visitors anymore. Who wants to see an old woman? I certainly wouldn't if I had a choice!"

Julia's laughter came easily to her, much easier than it was for her to walk into the living room and sit down. She extended an arthritic hand toward Connor and Sarah to do the same. "Yes, my hands are a terrible mess. Been suffering with these nasty things for years now, but it's getting worse. Makes keeping a house up much more of a chore than it used to be and since my Frankie passed away, well, I just try to make do. I know God won't give me any more than I can handle."

Sarah scanned the walls of the home which were primarily covered with black-and-white photos of people who were likely family who she had never known.

"Who was Frankie?" Connor asked.

"Oh, God rest his soul, he was my husband of fifty-seven years, a wonderful man. Family moved to Montana from Brooklyn. Italian family—must have been a hundred of them. Big, loud bunch of characters. They owned a restaurant in Helena. Fantastic food. That's where we met. I was going to college there. Frankie loved to cook for me. He served in the Navy during Korea. That's where he met a fellow soldier who offered to sell Frankie his family feed store business here in Baggs. We kept that store running through good times and bad until he died of a heart attack five years ago. Now I just live off the Social Security and me and Mr. Whiskers keep each other company. Enough about this old woman's story, though. I just have to hear about you wanting to see my brother, the ornery old fool."

Sarah leaned forward. "Julia, when was the last time you saw Hap?"

Mr. Whiskers had jumped up onto Julia's lap, purring loudly as the old woman lightly scratched under his chin. "Oh, goodness, it's been a while. I know his health isn't so good. Heard about the stroke, but I haven't even seen him since then. I can't drive and getting someone to take me out, well, it's tough. My church picks me up on Sundays so I can attend services and a group of them makes sure I have groceries each week. As for seeing my brother, I guess it was January's funeral some ten years ago. My goodness, has it really been that long?"

"So, he lives alone, like you?"

Julia turned and looked at Connor. "I believe so, yes. He never was one for having people around. He's a good man but can be difficult at times. I recall an elementary school teacher of his giving him low marks, saying 'doesn't play well with others'. Yes, that would be my brother all right. Especially if he thinks you've done him wrong—watch out!"

Connor followed up with another question. "And where he lives, that's the family ranch where you grew up as well?"

Julia nodded as her eyes lit up with happy memories of a childhood long gone. "Yes. It was a tough place but such beauty. The winters could be very cold, the summers very hot, and food was not something we took for granted. But, all in all, I loved growing up there. Hap was the horseman of the family. Since he was young, he always had this connection with horses, a quiet strength those incredibly powerful animals seemed to respect. My

71

brother had almost no patience for people, but I would watch him work with a horse for hours, days, and weeks at a time. He was not yet a teenager and people were bringing wild colts to the ranch for him to break. It was truly something to see.

"He had his reputation for toughness even then. There was this time, Hap couldn't have been more than ten or eleven years old, and he saw these three older boys picking on a girl walking by wearing a pair of glasses. Now back then glasses weren't nearly so common as they are today. They were calling her four-eyes, coke bottle, typical bully behavior and they had surrounded her so she couldn't just walk away. I was watching from the other side of the street and saw Hap's eyes get that fire in them when his temper went hot. He stood there glowering over at those boys picking on that poor girl. And then he tells me to wait where I was and walks right across that street toward those boys and tells them to knock it off and leave the girl alone.

"I could tell they were all confused by this kid who seemed not to be intimidated by them in the least. Then the biggest one, I think he was one of the McManus kids, they had a farm about ten miles from our ranch, he makes his way over to Hap and pushes my brother hard in the chest. Almost knocked him down. Well, Hap steps on over and pushes the bigger boy right back. Hap might have looked like a skinny bit of bones and skin, but he was strong. Our father would tell him to pick something up just to see if he could, and more often than not, Hap seemed to find the strength to do it.

"He wasn't strong enough to take on three older boys at once, though, and that's just what happened. I stood frozen in my spot across the street and watched the other two boys grab onto my brother from behind while the other one punched Hap in the gut. Knocked the air out of him and those boys were pointing and laughing for a second or two, but Hap got right back up and started swinging. They weren't laughing any more. Hap was knocked down again and again and each time he was back up throwing punches at the three of them. He got in some good shots, too.

"Finally, those boys had enough. They backed away from Hap, yelled that he was crazy, but then when Hap started coming at them again, they turned and ran. My brother was busted up pretty bad, had a cheek swollen up like a grapefruit, an ear all scratched and bleeding, and he was limping from a twisted ankle, and every one of his knuckles was scraped from when one of his punches found its mark.

"All the way home, and it was a long walk for us from town to home, Hap was looking down at those knuckles and grinning. Scraped up knuckles, that pretty much was how I saw my brother back then. When he saw something he didn't think was right he'd come out swinging. In fact, there was something that involved your mother Shirley that fits with that very thing. It was the time I saw Hap and realized there was something in him that scared me. It was the very same thing that might have been part of what attracted your grandmother to him in the first place, but just as likely frightened her, too."

Now Connor was the one leaning forward, as fascinated by Julia's stories of her brother, their grandfather, as Sarah was. "What did you see that scared you so much?" he asked.

Julia Wilkes cleared her throat. She looked at both Connor and Sarah and then nodded. "Okay, I'll tell you what I saw that night. Shirley and Hap were already together. I was up visiting, me and Frankie, after hearing January had left my brother to go live with her family. I had never seen Hap so happy and relaxed as he was with Shirley. He was talking, laughing, and always watching over her. Frankie remarked to me the age difference. Hap was about fifteen years older and like your grandmother at the time, still legally married, but I thought little of it. Both of them were adults and it seemed that for the first time in his life, my brother was completely content.

"One night, we all made the drive down to a bar in Glendive. It was Frankie's idea. He hated how quiet the ranch was. He liked people, music, and dancing. I was more surprised with how quickly Hap agreed to the idea. Apparently, him and Shirley had been going out dancing for weeks together, something I don't think my brother or January had ever done.

"So, this bar, it was a bit rough. A mix of farmers, truckers, and on this night, a group of bikers were in for a visit as well. I suggested we leave, but Frankie shrugged it off and Shirley and Hap both said we could stay for a little bit and see how it went. Your grandmother was cute as a button. Her dark hair was made up perfect and those big brown eyes of hers. Well, I'm sure more than a few heads were turning her way when she walked in with Hap. Not that my brother wasn't a good-looking man as well. He was, but he also sent out an unspoken signal that he didn't care to be bothered and he wasn't interested in anyone but Shirley. I imagine some women go their whole lives not knowing what it feels like to have a man's complete attention like that.

"Now, here's something few people know about my brother. He loves the music of Waylon Jennings and on this night him and Shirley had a dance to a Waylon Jennings song about an outlaw— that slow one with the curse word in the title. I watched the two of them dancing with one another, Hap holding Shirley's hand in his, as they moved slowly around the dance floor, and I could see my brother singing the words to her and Shirley smiling as she rested her head on his shoulder. I knew then that those two were very much in love. The year they spent together, it was no fling, or some temporary distraction. Hap loved your grandmother very much and she loved him just the same.

"Well, the song finishes. Hap excuses himself to use the bathroom and Shirley says she will get us some more drinks while we are waiting at the table. Now, I knew right off that was a bad idea and told Frankie to go with her. He kind of rolled his eyes at me and then gets up to follow Shirley to the bar, but she's already there making the order. By then, one of the biker fellas, a big long-haired bearded guy, looks just like they do in those biker movies, he's trying to talk up Shirley, putting his hand on her back and rubbing her shoulders. She keeps leaning away from him and he keeps moving closer. Frankie gets there and he tries to step between the biker and your grandma, but the biker isn't having it and shoulders Frankie to the side while keeping his hand on Shirley's back. I knew if my brother walked out and saw this there would be trouble.

"I'm kind of frozen in my seat, trying to decide if I should get up or not, when Shirley gets mad and twists away from the biker. Frankie tries to step between them again, but two other bikers push him back while the other guy, the one who took a liking to your grandma, he reaches out and grabs her by the arm and pulls her back to him, hard enough I can see Shirley's face wince in pain. She cries out and then there's just this blur racing across the room and I know it's Hap, and I know his eyes got that fire again, just like when he was a kid, and he comes out swinging.

"He hit that biker so hard with the first punch, I thought the man's head was gonna fly off his body. You could hear the horrible sound of it, like a big, wet towel dropping onto the floor. Hap's fists kept right on punching faster and faster. The biker fell and Hap was on him like a wild animal, those knuckles of his slamming into the man's head and face. He must have hit him ten or twenty times before two other bikers managed to pull Hap off. And then my brother was on them too and I could see his eyes, all lit up with rage and fury, and the bikers backed off. By then the bar owner was yelling out he had called the police and the ranchers and truckers, and other locals had positioned themselves between Hap and the bikers, trying to keep them separated.

"That's when I saw Shirley looking up at my brother as he stood there wild-eyed, fists clenching and unclenching, seeming at that time to only want more confrontation. I could tell she was uncertain how she felt about what had just happened. You see, a woman wants to feel safe and protected, but at the same time, a man who can give those things to her can also be dangerous. I think Shirley was realizing the darker potential of Hap's nature and it scared her a bit. She loved the man, but on that night, she also saw the monster."

The room went quiet, the silence interrupted only by the cat's purring, and then another question from Sarah. "My grandma left us a letter after she died which said that she and Hap split up after January decided to give the marriage another try. Is that true?"

Julia frowned a little while gently rubbing the tops of her arthritic fingers. "It could be. I wasn't around then but heard some of it from friends I still had in Savage who kept me updated. My brother wouldn't talk about it and January and me never cared for each other. I always felt she was a bit of a b-word. I did hear that Hap had told Shirley he would meet with her to talk one last time before she left for good. In fact, I think it was to be at the same bar I just told you the story about.

"Apparently, he never made it there, though. Nobody would have known about it, but January bragged to someone in town she had Hap back under her control and that she had made him break a promise to that 'silly girl" and left her waiting for him at the bar. That was January's way. She had a long streak of cruel in her. I asked Hap about it a few years later, but he shut down, refused to talk about it and I knew not to press him. He never mentioned Shirley again and we grew more distant, talking less and less as the years went by. In fact, the last time I spent any *real* amount of time with him was at Henry's funeral."

Both Connor and Sarah glanced at each other before Connor spoke again. "Who is Henry?"

Julia's cat suddenly decided it was time to leave, jumping off the couch and disappearing into another room. "Henry was the boy Hap and January had adopted shortly after Shirley left. I only saw him a few times but heard plenty of stories. He hated living on the ranch, hated animals, the work, the solitude, and was always running away. Henry had been a troubled child and by the time he was a young man, those troubles seemed to overtake him completely. I know people talk about the importance of nurture, but you know sometimes nature is going to win out and Henry's nature was that of a very unhappy person. He died at nineteen of a drug overdose. Some campers found his body in a wooded area outside Missoula. He had been dead for weeks. The animals had already taken most of him.

"After that, whatever love Hap and January might have had between them, if any had ever really existed, was long gone. The only time anyone saw them together was during Sunday service and even then, it was clear to anyone paying attention the relationship was one of convenience and habit. When January became sick, Hap cared for her as best he could and planned on burying her with our family on the hill, Vaughn's Hill, that overlooks the property. Her family refused, though, saying she deserved better. Hap was beyond fighting much of anything at that point and let them take her body back to Helena for the service and burial.

"I sat next to my brother during that service and fought back tears the whole time. Not for January's loss mind you, but for how empty my brother seemed. It was as if everything inside of him had been sucked out over the years. His eyes were vacant, empty. He was just the shell of the brother I once knew. I figure most at the funeral thought he was broken up about January dying, but I knew better. Hap was finally realizing all the time that had been lost, how so little of that time was left to him, and that he had made a terrible mistake in letting your grandmother go. I could feel that pain coming off him and knew there was nothing to be done about it and that made me feel so bad for him. I had been blessed to have many years with the love of my life, my Frankie, but Hap had turned his back on that kind of love, turned his back on Shirley. Knowing that left him broken."

"Did Hap know about our dad?"

Julia let Connor's question float between them unanswered for a moment as she considered her response. "Yes, I believe so. I know he knew of the possibility of your father because I told him about it personally years ago. I kept tabs on Shirley for a while. I heard she had given birth to a son and it didn't take what little math skills I have to figure out that boy had to be my brother's. So, I told him about it and he just did what he always would when confronted with something he didn't want to hear. He shut down, ignored it, and moved on. Hap didn't have the courage to find out for himself and sadly Shirley was likely still too hurt to tell him about their boy. Months turn to years, she finds another man, and life just goes on with the truth getting buried under the past."

"I think that's such crap. Shame on the both of them."

Julia nodded her sad agreement. "You're right, Sarah. You're absolutely right to feel that way. At least Shirley finally let you two know. She must have felt terrible not having done so sooner, to give your father a chance to know the truth as well before he and your mother were killed in that car accident. Say, do you have a picture of your father?"

Sarah nodded as she reached into a pocket of her jacket and withdrew a small color photo of her parents, which she then handed to Julia. The old woman held the photograph up to her face and gave a smile that was both pain and pleasure.

"They look so happy. And your dad, I can certainly see Hap in him—the same build and facial features. I see Shirley as well. What was your mother's name?"

Connor's reply was a low whisper. He still found it hard to talk about his parents' death. "Jessica. Her name was Jessica."

Julia sensed Connor's pain and felt her own eyes welling with tears.

"She was beautiful," Julia said. "Like the both of you. I'm so glad you came here today."

The sound of a ringing telephone cried out from the kitchen.

"Just a minute while I get that." Julia rose slowly from the couch, letting out a soft groan as she did so, and then shuffled her way to the phone, which required her to use both hands to pick up.

"Hello? Who is this? Please speak up. Uh-huh. Oh, I see. Is he going to be all right? Oh my. Okay. Thank you for letting me know, Sheriff. Goodbye."

After returning the phone to its cradle, Julia looked both confused and frightened. "That was the Richland County Sheriff, from Montana. Hap is in the hospital. He had some kind of attack and the sheriff isn't sure he'll make it."

Both Connor and Sarah stood up from the couch, realizing at the same moment that the purpose of their trip might be dying in a hospital bed hundreds of miles away.

CHAPTER 12

"Mr. Wilkes, what do you think you're doing?"

Hap was in no mood to explain. He just wanted to go home. The nurse had found him pulling his catheter right before he started to do the same to the IV drip.

"No, Mr. Wilkes, don't do that. Stop it!"

Hap yanked the IV out and glared back at the nurse, his chin jutting out in defiance. "I'm not dying in here ma'am, so you best move out of my way."

Hap stood up from the bed, and then was temporarily overcome with a wave of dizziness and nausea. He felt the nurse trying to gently force him back down, but instead she only pushed his anger and frustration to another level. "Get your damn hands off me. Call the sheriff, tell him to get his ass out here and take me home. Go on. Do it."

Milly, the supervising nurse, entered the room. She was a tall, broad- shouldered woman whose wide face communicated a no-nonsense attitude that was accustomed to having patients and other nurses follow her orders.

"Mr. Wilkes, if I need to force you to lie back down, I will."

Hap grunted at the other nurse's threat as he made his way toward the hallway outside his room. "I have every right to check myself out. Now call the sheriff and tell him I'll be waiting outside."

When Milly placed her large hands on each of Hap's shoulders to hold him in place, the rancher's eyes flared, and his lips drew back in a snarl. "Ma'am, please don't do that. I don't want trouble here, but if you don't get out of my way, trouble *is* coming. More trouble than you care to deal with."

Milly looked at the other nurse and then shrugged her shoulders, her hands falling away from Hap as she did so. "Okay, Mr. Wilkes, you want to leave this hospital you go right on ahead, but you'll be signing a release before you do it understood?"

Hap was already past the door, his bad leg dragging behind him. "Fine, give me whatever I need to sign and then leave me be. Where's my boots?"

As Hap moved down the hallway toward the exit the back of his hospital gown flared open, a condition for which he indicated little concern over, but that had both nurses shaking their heads and trying not to laugh.

"I said where's my damn boots?"

An hour later found Hap sitting silently in the passenger seat of the sheriff's cruiser. He still wore the hospital gown while his feet were back inside of his beloved and much-worn cowboy boots and his hat once again sat atop his head.

"Mr. Wilkes, you are one big pain in my ass," Dillon said.

Hap said nothing as he looked out the passenger window while wondering how far they were from his ranch. After another ten minutes of silence he mumbled a question to the sheriff.

"You let them go onto my property?"

Dillon gripped the steering wheel a little tighter, knowing the rancher wouldn't like the answer. "Yes, they conducted their site evaluation. I had no authority to deny them that access. They're gone now so there's no need to get yourself worked up about it."

"Are they coming back?"

Dillon kept his eyes locked onto the road. "I don't know. They'll review the information they gathered and then get back to us when they're ready."

Hap turned to look directly at the sheriff. His voice seethed with rage. "And just what was it they gathered from *my* property, Sheriff? They find the excuse they need to slaughter those horses? Is that it?"

The sheriff took a deep breath. They were no more than ten minutes from Hap's ranch.

"I don't know, Mr. Wilkes. It's the government so it may take them another year or more before we hear back."

Hap shook his head and frowned. "No, I don't think so, Sheriff. Not this time. That fed, the little guy, he strikes me as the kind who will move right quick when it comes to taking something that isn't his."

Dillon knew Hap was right. He had picked up the exact same feeling from Bill Tuttle. Bureaucracy seemed to have a way of breeding jerks like him and lately there seemed to be more and more of them.

"Tell me, Sheriff, when the push comes to the shove, and it will, which side of the line are you gonna be standing on—mine or the feds? When I'm pointing a gun at them will I see you pointing yours right back at me?"

Dillon clenched his jaw, unable to reply to Hap's question because he wasn't yet sure of the answer. He was sworn to uphold the law, but at what point did that law become a crime?

CHAPTER 13

Connor and Sarah reached the hospital in Culbertson just a few hours after the sheriff and Hap had left. The receptionist informed them Hap had checked himself out and was likely already back home.

While disappointed they had missed him, Connor and his sister were also relieved to hear he was okay and knew they were less than an hour from the ranch.

"Should we just show up?" Connor said. "Or try to get the number and call him first to let him know we're coming?"

Sarah looked up from the photograph she had been staring at since Julia had given it to them right before they backed the Impala out from her driveway. It was a black and white picture of Grandma Shirley and Hap sitting atop two beautiful horses. In the background was the large hill Julia said was named after her grandfather, Vaughn Wilkes. She explained to them how that hill had always been Hap's favorite place in the world and was also home to a small family cemetery. Julia had left instructions in her will to be buried there herself when the time came, along with the urn that contained the ashes of her Frankie.

"When you make it to the ranch, give this picture to Hap. Tell him I was the one who gave it to you and that he's to treat you two like the family you are. Let him know that if I hear otherwise,

I'll come up there myself to set him right. I took that picture and remember it like it was yesterday."

Sarah was fascinated by the photograph. Though she had seen pictures of her grandma as a younger woman, Shirley had never appeared so vibrant and beautiful as she did while riding the horse next to Hap. As for Hap, Sarah could understand her grandmother's attraction to him. Even the two-dimensional photograph could not hide the natural confidence and determination that emanated from him. Sarah recalled her father Dex had a similar aura that had likely played a considerable part in her mother's attraction to him as well.

In the photo, neither Hap nor Shirley was looking at the camera, but rather had their eyes locked on one another, a small, knowing smile on each of their faces.

So that's what real love looks like. It was a phrase Sarah had repeated silently to herself as Connor drove the last few hundred miles of the journey to Savage.

The Impala passed a sign indicating Savage was just twelve miles ahead. Sarah looked down at the GPS and noted the address for the Wilkes home was just over twenty miles from their location.

Are you watching over us, Grandma Shirley?

Connor reached over to turn the Impala's radio on, working the dial to try and get a station, but he only succeeded in pulling up static. Tired of the sound, Sarah pushed his hand away from the radio.

"Let me try."

The speakers continued to buzz the angry sound of nothingness until finally, toward the very end of the dial, a slow, somewhat ominous sounding song came in. It was a country tune from decades ago, yet somehow it seemed familiar to both of them, but they couldn't yet figure out why.

"I'm for law and order, the way that it should be. This song is about the night they spent protecting you from me…"

The car's interior was filled with the music of a song Hap and Shirley had danced to together all those years ago—the very same dance Julia Wilkes had described to them earlier that day. Once the song was finished the station announcer's voice broke in.

"That was Waylon Jennings' *Outlaw*. Boy do we miss that man's music. They just don't make them like him anymore."

Both Connor and Sarah looked at one another, their eyes wide, finally realizing the song was the one Julia had just told them about.

"That's the song! Oh my gosh, Connor. What are the odds of that song playing right now?"

Connor shook his head, somewhat unsettled at the seemingly impossible coincidence. "I'll admit that's pretty weird."

Sarah turned off the radio and glanced down at the GPS. It was ten miles to the home of Hap Wilkes.

Ten miles to the grandfather they have never known.

Ten miles to a place that set into motion the events that led their existence.

Sarah looked out her window, noting the vast expanse of open fields, sensing how the geography naturally communicated it to be a place where freedom and possibility were as integral to the people who called these lands home as was the air that they breathed.

A place of seemingly endless new beginnings.

While Connor and Sarah completed the final few miles of their trip, Hap Wilkes slept in the family chair that had been brought over from Ireland by his grandfather Vaughn. It was a piece of furniture that had once, for the only time in his life, caused him to nearly strike a woman in anger.

January had always loathed the chair, thinking it a grotesque, dirty thing that should have been thrown out long ago. For Hap, as it had been to all the members of his family through generations, the chair represented the determined struggles for a better life. Struggles that included escaping the often-violent conflicts of Ireland, the long and perilous journey across the United States, and to finally making their home in the wild open expanses of eastern Montana. The chair had been handmade from Irish silver birch by a friend of the family when the Wilkes still lived in their native Ireland. It was a gift to Hap's great grandfather, Talbot, upon his marriage to Shannon Collins, the woman who would later encourage her son Vaughn's journey to America.

It was perhaps the only time in all the years Hap was with January, that he told her in no uncertain terms she was not to disobey his wishes. That chair was to remain in its place, not to be moved by her or anyone else.

Shortly after telling her so, January sold the chair.

Hap came back into the house and immediately saw the empty space near the small wood stove where the chair had been placed decades earlier by his grandfather. He looked up to see January smirking at him from the nearby kitchen, holding a cigarette in her hand, seeming to dare him to challenge her.

"Where is it?"

January shrugged her indifference at the question, rolling her eyes at Hap to let him know how little she thought of him. "I told you, that old thing needed to go. I called a thrift shop owner and he took it off our hands. Gave me ten dollars for it."

When January's eyes settled on Hap, she finally realized the danger. Her long-suffering husband looked back at her with smoldering fury, his hands clenched as the corner of his upper lip trembled. Hap moved across the living room toward her as his powerful right hand rose up over his head.

January was a hard woman, though, and not easily taken by fear. She quickly recovered from her uncertainty in the face of Hap's anger and sneered back at him. "Go ahead, Hap. Hit a woman. Hit your wife. That'll go fine with your well-earned reputation with the other inbred hillbillies around here. You'll prove to my family you're the man they said you were all along. You're nothing! That chair was just like you—a useless piece of garbage."

Hap stood frozen. He lowered his hand at the same moment he lowered his eyes.

"Just tell me who you sold it to, January. You can keep the money. I don't care about that."

Satisfied she had broken her husband, January let out an exaggerated sigh and shook her head in disgust. "All this for a stupid chair? Do you really have so little in this life that you would act like a spoiled child over a ratty old chair? It was the thrift store along Highway 107. The man's name is Arlo. Do you really intend to drive all the way out there to get it back?"

Hap turned around and walked out. Thirty minutes later he was negotiating with Arlo Greeves for the purchase of the chair January had just sold him.

Greeves was an affable fifty-two-year-old widower and generally well liked among the locals. He had run his small pawn shop for the last twenty-six years, doing his best to help the farming families acquire a little cash to get by during the lean times. Arlo made little profit himself from these transactions, but instead, was merely happy with the satisfaction of knowing he was helping others.

"Well look here, it's the Irish cowboy! Don't think I've ever seen you step foot in my store, Mr. Wilkes. You're being here so soon after Mrs. Wilkes sold me that chair today leads me to believe I'm now smack dab in the middle of a genuine domestic dispute."

Hap issued a thin, pained smile and nodded. "Yeah, it's something like that. I need my chair back, Mr. Greeves."

Arlo grimaced as he folded his arms across his chest. "Well, the thing is, Mr. Wilkes, I already have a buyer for that chair of yours. Gentleman from Sydney who owns an antique shop. I described the chair to him and he's on his way right now to pick it up. I can't rightly back out of the deal now. It wouldn't be fair."

"I said I need my chair back. I'm not leaving here without it."

Arlo smiled, trying to calm the rancher down. "I understand you're being upset, Mr. Wilkes. But, like I said, the man is already on his way here. I'm sorry, but I have a reputation for being a businessman of my word and I gave my word to him that the chair was his. We agreed to a price and the deal was done."

Hap stepped toward the counter behind which Arlo was standing. "Where's my chair? Don't make me ask again. I'll pay you back the ten dollars, okay? I just want what's mine."

Arlo looked up to see a newer Cadillac pulling off the highway and into one of the pawn shop parking spaces next to Hap's truck.

"I'm sorry, Mr. Wilkes. That there happens to be the new owner of the chair right now. I'd be happy to offer you a real good deal on one of the other chairs I have available."

Hap's temper finally broke open like the gates of hell, out of which flew the righteous indignation of a man whose patience had reached its limit. A single ten-dollar bill was slammed onto the top of Arlo's counter, after which Hap pushed himself past the shop owner and into the back area where he found his chair waiting.

Arlo picked up the phone and dialed the Sheriff's Office, telling a then much younger Adeline Rhodes that he was being robbed by Hap Wilkes. Adeline assured Arlo that Sheriff Potts was on his way.

By the time Hap was carrying the chair to the door its intended new owner, an older white-haired man named Robert Town, was walking in. Robert, believing Hap was an employee of Arlo's, pointed toward his Cadillac.

"The trunk is already open. You can put the chair right in there. Hold up a minute, though, and let me get a good look at her."

Hap mumbled a profanity under his breath and moved past the older man on his way to his truck, causing Town to look over at Arlo. "What the hell is going on here, Mr. Greeves? I thought we had a deal?"

Arlo moved out from behind the counter and tried to assure the buyer he intended to stay true to the agreed to deal, which unknown to Hap, was the sale of his family chair to the man from Sydney for forty dollars. "Yes sir, Mr. Town, we *do* have a deal. That man there was the *former* owner of the chair and he seems to be confused in thinking he still owns it. The sheriff is already on his way and we'll have this all sorted out in no time."

Robert's eyes narrowed as he looked Arlo up and down. "That chair isn't stolen is it? I don't buy stolen goods you know. I run a reputable business."

Arlo shook his head vigorously from side to side, dismayed anyone would suggest such a possibility. "Absolutely not, Mr. Town! I have the purchase receipt! That man's wife sold it to me

91

herself. And as you can see that chair is a beautiful piece. With just a bit of refurbishing it should make a wonderful addition to your inventory."

Robert looked from Arlo to Hap, who was by then already putting the chair into the back of his truck. "Seems that man has other ideas, Mr. Greeves."

Just then, Sheriff Stan Potts pulled his car in front of Hap's pickup and got out. Unlike his son Dillon, who would succeed him as sheriff years later and take a more diplomatic, work-it out-approach to the job, Stan Potts enjoyed a widely accepted reputation as a man who took nothing from anyone—ever. When it came to Sheriff Stan Potts most residents of Richland County, Montana figured if the sheriff told you to do it, you damn well better. A sign hung just behind his desk that read, "*Shut your damn pie hole*" and that's what most did whenever Stan Potts was around.

Hap Wilkes, though, happened to *not* be included among those who feared the hard-nosed sheriff. He liked Stan well enough, having known him as far back as shared school days, but the rancher also had a natural suspicion of anyone who went around with a badge and a gun, and so, their relationship had inevitably changed over the years to one of tepid mutual respect. That relationship was then sorely tested the day January Wilkes sold her husband's chair to Arlo Greeves.

CHAPTER 14

"Mr. Tuttle, the senator would consider this a personal favor to him. We very much want to open that land to our friends at Greenex. We're talking a number of high-paying, green-friendly jobs, and we'd be more than happy to make certain your efforts were looked upon favorably by some very influential people—the kind of people who could help to deliver you a significant promotion."

Tuttle could hardly contain his excitement, believing his work in transferring the Wilkes property over to the Bureau of Land Management might get him a high-ranking position in Washington D.C.

"Well, Mr. Tyrell please let the senator know everything is proceeding ahead of schedule. We've submitted the endangered species report, which I will then have fast-tracked. We also stumbled upon something unexpected during the site visit which will work in our favor as well."

Anthony Tyrell leaned forward. "Do tell, Mr. Tuttle.

Tuttle folded his small hands in front of him and grinned. "An unlicensed family cemetery. There are four graves that appear to be for two men and two women on the upper-northeast corner of the hill. It seems the Wilkes family has been burying their own on the property. We've already completed a search of the Richland County records and found no documentation of any government approval for the site. I then had staff conduct a review of state records and the very same thing—no approval. Now, given the soon-to-be land status of the property being designated an endangered species site and its proximity to a major river, I think we might have even more leverage over Mr. Wilkes than originally believed."

Anthony Tyrell, who had been working as an adviser for longtime Montana Senator Burton Mansfield for the last three years, smiled back at Tuttle while nodding his approval. The senator was among the most powerful figures in Congress and still young enough to make a run for president, something the very ambitious forty-three-year-old Tyrell intended to be an integral part of.

"Very good, Mr. Tuttle. I will be sure to let the senator know as well as our Greenex contacts. How soon do you think before we can begin construction of the wind turbines on that hill?"

Tuttle held up two pork sausage fingers. "Shouldn't be more than a month or two. I'll be sending someone out to the property with notifications in hand and I've already approved the contract for elimination of the horses, which will take place next week."

The senate adviser's eyes widened. "That soon?"

Tuttle chuckled. "Yeah, I know the wheels of government have a reputation for moving slowly, but when there's some real motivation involved, we can go in and do whatever we damn well please before anyone is the wiser. That's what I intend to do in getting the senator's Greenex friends the access they want to the Wilkes property. It'll be a couple months at most. You'll see."

Tyrell stood up, buttoned the front of his navy-blue dress suit, adjusted his dark-red tie, and then extended his hand. "That's fantastic, Mr. Tuttle. You're going to make some very important people very happy. Oh, about the horses. Do you really think it necessary to kill them? It was my understanding the BLM normally auctions wild horses to the highest bidder."

Tuttle shook his head. "No, that's mostly public relations. It would be too cost prohibitive to do that every time we needed to clear out an area of some herd. You must capture the things, transport them, pay staff for the auction . . . it really starts to add up. It's far simpler to just kill them all at once and be done with hit. Like I said, we can go in and do whatever we damn well please before anyone is the wiser. Besides, I never liked horses—too dumb and too big."

CHAPTER 15

"What's going on, Hap?"

The rancher looked up to see the sheriff staring at him, his right hand casually resting on the butt of his sidearm.

"Just getting my chair back, Sheriff. I'll be on my way now."

Stan tilted his head to the side, trying to measure just how upset the rancher was, which in turn would tell him how much was involved in getting him to stay put. "Hold on there just a minute, Hap. I got a call saying you were robbing Mr. Greeves. Something about a missing chair, which I'll assume is that chair sitting in the back of your truck."

Hap spit to the side and then glared back at his childhood friend. "That's a damn lie, Stan and you know it. This here chair has been in my family before either of us were alive."

The sheriff leaned over the back of Hap's truck to get a closer look. "So, how did it come to be in Mr. Greeves's possession?"

Hap's wide shoulders slumped slightly while his voice lowered to a whisper. "January sold it to him. I told her not to, but she done it anyways while I was out of the house. The woman, she can be a stubborn cold one. I already gave Arlo his ten dollars back so I figure we're all square and I can just take my chair home with me where it belongs."

The sheriff tried to hide his smile. He sensed Hap's embarrassment at having to admit his wife was currently making such a mess of his life. "So, this here is just a misunderstanding between you and January. Is that what you're telling me?"

Hap realized he had become a source of amusement for the sheriff and felt his temper rising within him once again as a result. "I think it best I be on my way, Sheriff before I kick your ass into the dirt like I done before."

Stan knew exactly what Hap was referring to. Many years ago, when they were just two rambunctious juniors in high school, Hap Wilkes and Stan Potts took a liking for the same girl. Her name was Pearl Young, and she was the youngest daughter of the then Richland County administrator. Both young men had met her at a county schools dance held at the Sydney Grange and had become equally infatuated by her long blonde hair, easy smile, and hourglass figure.

Most boys of seventeen suffer from a sense of immortality and indestructibility, and Hap and Stan weren't exceptions to that rule. The eventual conflict over winning the favors of the young and beautiful Pearl Young was inevitable.

As for Pearl, she quite enjoyed having the two tall, handsome young men vying for her attentions. So much so that she actively advertised for the clash of fists that resulted, telling both boys if they wanted to go steady with her, they were to fight it out and she would be there to declare the winner.

And so, the challenge was made. Hap and Stan were to meet at high noon behind the large water tower that once stood across the road from where Arlo Greeves's pawn shop still resided. Every boy and girl from twenty miles around tried to make it to that fight. Some older kids who had cars came from as far away as Billings. By the time Stan and Hap stood ten paces apart glaring back at each other, nearly two hundred looked on, urging the two boys to give it their best.

Pearl, enjoying the spotlight far more than either Hap or Stan, walked slowly and quite dramatically to the center of the large circle the crowd of young people had created, holding a cream-colored scarf in her hand. She had spent all morning preparing her hair and choosing just the right outfit, a dark blue dress that barely contained the ample bounty that was her chest and as she stood there holding out the scarf, Pearl could barely contain her excitement at the idea that all of this was being done for her.

"Boys," she said. "When I drop this scarf, the fight begins. Good luck to the both of you."

If a poll of the crowd had been taken at that time most would have favored Stan Potts as the one to emerge victorious. He was a well- known athlete and a far more high-profile student. Hap, on the other hand, while clearly a confident young man, was more solitary, spending his free time alone riding horses around the Wilkes property rather than engaging in the social activities of school. Stan was also both slightly taller and of a heavier build than Hap.

As the scarf fell and Pearl scrambled to get out of the way, her eyes shimmered with excitement at the violence to come. Stan threw the first few punches, two of which found their mark against Hap's nose and mouth.

The young rancher's head snapped back and then Hap grinned as he tasted his own blood on his tongue. Stan was strong, but not strong enough, and that grin was Hap's way of letting Stan know it.

Stan looked back at Hap's grinning and bloodied face and feared the same thing. Most boys after being hit like that would have quit right then, but Hap seemed to somehow have grown stronger.

The someday sheriff threw several more punches, hoping for a quick knock-out blow. Hap ducked and moved, but didn't yet punch back, causing some of the observers to jeer that he was too chicken to fight.

Stan grew desperate, realizing he was already growing tired, while also sensing Hap could likely go on for several hours more. Working a ranch from dawn to dusk had a way of developing strength and endurance that could never be replicated on a football field.

It was at that moment Stan thought if he could grab a hold of Hap, he might be able to take him down onto the ground and smother him enough so that he couldn't continue. He suddenly charged and was rewarded with a collision that resulted in Hap falling backwards with Stan on top of him.

The crowd roared its approval, including a lusty shout from Pearl.

Stan was familiar with the phrase, *catch a tiger by the tail*, but on that day, he discovered firsthand its true meaning. Stan could feel Hap's power beneath him and knew then he was truly in trouble. The young rancher's body was like a tightly wound, unbreakable rope, and within seconds, Hap had rolled Stan over and loomed above him, his fists raining down onto Stan's face and chest as a thought kept repeating itself in Stan's mind.

Damn he hits hard.

Each blow from Hap was like a hammer and they came one after the other until finally Pearl cried out to stop it as some of the older boys who had been watching pulled Hap off, leaving Stan barely moving and bloodied on the ground. Pearl knelt down next to him and attempted to clean the blood from his face with the same scarf used to begin the fight. She then looked back at Hap with disgust.

"What is wrong with you? You're like some kind of animal."

Hap realized then that Pearl had merely used both him and Stan for her own amusement. That realization led Hap to simply shrug his agreement at the accusation from a girl he now saw as all too typically self-involved.

"Yeah, I'm like some kind of animal."

Hap wiped some of his own blood from his mouth and nose and walked slowly toward Pearl and then took that hand and lightly brushed it across the frightened girl's face, leaving a dark crimson trail across her cheek. He then looked down at Stan Potts while nodding at Pearl.

"She's all yours."

And with that, Hap Wilkes began the long walk back home.

Both men recalled that decades-ago confrontation as they now stood facing each other once again. Time had made Stan Potts the respected and feared sheriff of Richland County and Hap Wilkes a poor rancher dealing with a perpetually unhappy wife.

"Not so sure if we tangled up another time, the result would be the same, Hap."

Hap's eyes narrowed as he tried to determine how willing, if at all, the sheriff was in taking back the chair. "Maybe not, but here's the thing. This chair is mine. January had no right to sell it. I paid the man back. Now, I'm going home."

Robert Town moved down from the entrance steps of Arlo's pawn shop and pointed at Hap. "I heard that man threaten you, Sheriff. Said he was going to kick your ass in the dirt. Is that kind of talk legal around here?"

Sheriff Potts closed his eyes. *Damn. Now I got to hold up my reputation and make an example out of Hap.*

"Mr. Wilkes, I need you to turn around and place your hands on the hood of the truck."

Hap stared back at the sheriff in disbelief. "You can't be serious, Stan. This is *my* chair."

Behind Robert Town, Arlo Greeves ran back behind his counter and called Adeline Rhodes to tell her the Irish cowboy was refusing his arrest by the sheriff and that she better send backup.

"Mr. Wilkes, I won't ask again. Please turn around and put your hands on the hood of the truck—NOW."

Hap let out a long, slow sigh and shook his head. "Is this really how it's going to be, Sheriff? We both know you're arresting me just to save face."

Stan's hand rested on the butt of his holstered gun. "I'm just doing my job and you did threaten an officer of the law."

Hap waved a dismissive hand at the sheriff as the other hand reached out to open his truck door. "No, I was just reminding an old friend of something that happened between them a long time ago. Guess times have changed, huh?"

The sheriff drew his gun and pointed it at the rancher. "No, Hap, times haven't changed. We have. Now move away from the door and put your hands on the hood like I asked."

Hap watched the gun coming out of its holster and then looked back at Arlo Greeves who stood watching from the entrance of his shop. "Mr. Greeves, did I or did I not just pay you back the ten dollars you gave my wife for *my* chair?"

The pawn shop owner glanced at Robert Town and Sheriff Potts, before his eyes settled back onto Hap. "Yes, Mr. Wilkes, you did but—"

Hap cut off Arlo's remark. "And has this gentleman here actually paid you any money for the chair that you hoped to sell him?"

Arlo shook his head. "No, but—"

Again, Hap interrupted, his voice rising to a level much louder than his normally low, hoarse whisper. "Well there you go, Sheriff. I rest my case. Now, if you don't mind, I'm taking *my* chair back to *my* home and that is that."

Hap sat behind the wheel, started up the old Ford pickup and proceeded to drive off in a spray of gravel and dust, barely missing the arriving deputy's vehicle as he did so.

"Crackers on Sunday, Sheriff! Are you just gonna let him get away like that? I always heard you were a hard man who demanded respect."

Stan glared at Robert, causing the older man to take two steps backwards.

"Shut your pie hole, Mr. Town before you really piss me off."

CHAPTER 16

Sheriff Potts and his deputy, a younger man of twenty-five named Buck Hayes, had been following closely behind Hap's truck for the last several miles as the rancher made his way back to his home on the outskirts of Savage. Though both squad car lights were flashing furiously, Hap refused to pull over.

All this for a damn chair?

Even as he said it to himself, the sheriff knew it wasn't true. This was about much more than just the chair. January Wilkes had been pushing Hap's buttons for years. She believed herself better than most around Savage and loathed Hap for being the man who kept her here. Why the two had married always struck him as something of a mystery. The sheriff had seen more than enough during his time in law enforcement to know the phrase *young and dumb* was far from a simple cliché - it was an all too real and often unfortunate fact of life that trapped people into relationships they had no business hoping would someday work out.

The pickup truck turned off the main road and onto the long drive that marked the entrance to the Wilkes ranch. A big plume of dust billowed up from behind Hap's truck, nearly hiding the vehicle from the sheriff's view. Stan squinted through his windshield, growing both angrier and more concerned with how the situation would ultimately play out.

"Dammit to hell, Hap. What are you gonna make me do?"

A glance by the sheriff into his rearview mirror showed Deputy Hayes right behind him. *Hayes better keep his damn gun holstered. This ain't no time for hotshot wanna-be tough guys.*

The sheriff's concern over his deputy's demeanor was legitimate. Buck enjoyed the power that came with the badge and gun, while not always practicing the appropriate measure of calm responsibility that Stan knew made for the best kind of lawman. One should never go looking for a fight if a fight could be avoided.

Hap's truck moved through the large, unfenced front yard area where it came to a quick stop just a few paces from his front porch. Sheriff Potts made certain he stopped his own car at least twenty feet behind the truck, to make certain Deputy Hayes was left behind the sheriff's car. He knew the more distance between Buck and Hap, the better.

"Hap, I know you saw my lights. A citizen is required by law to pull the hell over. Why are you pushing this thing into something it doesn't have to be?"

Hap was already removing the chair from the back of his truck. He didn't respond. He was focused on January's fury as she bolted out from the front door.

"What the hell is this?" she yelled. "You have the law chasing you down? What did you go and do this time you stupid man?" January had placed herself between her husband and the entrance to their home with her hands on her hips.

"January, please get out of the way. I'm just putting my chair back inside where it belongs."

January moved toward Hap and jabbed a finger into his chest with enough force Sheriff Potts could hear it from where he stood by his vehicle.

"You are doing no such thing. Take that damn chair and leave it outside. The thing stinks of poverty and I won't have it in my house."

Hap stood motionless, staring into the eyes of a woman he thought perhaps, some time ago, to have once loved. What looked back at him was someone he no longer recognized.

"Woman, you need to move."

January slapped across Hap's face hard enough it made his eyes water. "You have no right to talk to me like that. No right at all."

"Hey! Mr. Wilkes, you step away from your wife. Right now. That's an order."

It was Deputy Hayes, seizing the chance to play hero. As Sheriff Potts turned to stop his deputy's approach, Buck scrambled to the other side of the sheriff's police cruiser, moving fast toward the rancher, his gun drawn.

Hap saw the weapon out of the corner of his eye—saw it pointing at both him and January. The stupidity of the deputy's actions, combined with the frustration of his wife's treatment of him, sent him into a full-blown rage.

The chair Hap held was thrown across the yard where it landed against Buck's chest, causing the deputy to tumble back. Hap moved nearly as quickly as the chair, landing atop the deputy, his hands encircling Buck's neck and squeezing with a strength few other men in the entire county possessed.

Buck looked up into the face of madness. Hap's eyes were like two hot coals, his lips pulled back in a savage snarl, and try as he might, the deputy was powerless to pull Hap's hands away from him. The rancher was simply too strong.

Sheriff Potts moved to pull Hap off his deputy while January screamed at the sight of her husband looking every bit like a man who was attempting the murder of another. She placed no blame on herself, though, instead thinking it was yet another example of Hap's stupidity. He was as dumb and brutish as the horses he chose to spend so much time with.

"Let him go," Stan yelled as he attempted to pull his childhood friend off, but his grip remained clamped around the other man's neck. The muscles of Hap's arms, shoulders, and back were as hard as the roots of a Montana cedar. Buck's face turned a mottled purple as his eyes rolled up into his skull.

Genuinely fearing for his deputy's life, Sheriff Potts drew his weapon, gripped it by the barrel and sent the butt of the gun cracking into the top of Hap's head. The blow opened a wound that created a stream of blood flowing over the rancher's face, making him appear like some demonic beast recently crawled out from the bowels of hell.

Hap kept choking Buck.

Again, the sheriff's gun came crashing down, this time causing Hap to topple to the side. Deputy Hayes gasped and coughed as he rolled over onto his hands and knees and threw up the contents of his lunch from earlier that day.

"Stay down, Hap," Stan said. "No more."

Finally, the rancher's madness dissipated. He looked through the blood that continued to seep from his head and over his eyes and grunted. "Are you taking me in, Sheriff?"

Stan nodded. His face was grim.

"You left me no choice. I have to arrest you for this."

Hap stood up on unsteady legs, felt the gash on his head, and winced. "Damn, are you still upset about that fight we had over Pearl Young?"

Stan chuckled, glad to have Hap sounding more like his old self. "Hardly. It's like I said. I'm just here doing a job."

Hap winced again from the throbbing pain in his head and then nodded. "Yeah, I suppose you are. Can I ask just one favor before you cuff me?"

"What's that?"

Hap walked slowly toward his recently thrown chair and picked it up. "Let me put this back in the house before we go."

Sheriff Potts looked at Hap and then January, who stood on the porch with her arms crossed over her chest. "Sure," he said. "Go ahead."

Hap half-lifted, half-dragged the chair back toward the house before pausing in front of his wife. "This chair better be here when I get back. I'm asking you as nice as I can. Please don't do anything to it."

After returning the chair Hap stepped onto the porch and stood in front of January. She glared up at him, and then, shocking both the sheriff and his deputy, proceeded to spit into her husband's face.

Hap said nothing as he wiped the spit and blood away, turned from January, and then held his hands out in front of him to be cuffed. Stan noted Hap's slumped shoulders and how he stared silently at the ground.

Hap was a man emotionally defeated, hanging on by what small thread of self-respect and dignity remained within him. Stan glared at January, looking at her with the same contempt she so willingly and repeatedly afforded her husband.

After instructing Deputy Hayes to place Hap into the back of his squad car the sheriff strode toward January, who stared at him with icy indifference. "Mrs. Wilkes, I would consider it a personal favor to me that you leave that chair alone for now, understood?"

January smirked and then shrugged. "Fine."

Stan took a deep breath while waiting for her to look up at him again. "There's one more thing, Mrs. Wilkes. Your husband will be sitting in my jail until you show up to pay the fine that I have no choice but to give him. Now I know you come from a family of some means so there's no reason this can't be taken care of soon. I don't want to see you letting Hap rot away in a cell out of spite. Whatever problems you two are having, you're a better woman than that. He'd do the same for you and I now expect you to do the same for him."

January's smirk widened into a wicked smile as her eyes lit up with mischief. "So, unless I pay his fine, Hap stays in jail? Is that right, Sheriff?"

Stan wagged a warning finger. "Don't you dare think about playing around with an idea like that. You push me, I'll be back around to arrest you myself. You come get your husband and work this out between you two like civilized folk."

"Perhaps some time in jail is what that stupid man needs, Sheriff. Maybe some common sense might sneak in between those rocks in his head. My husband is a silly, pathetic creature, and I might enjoy knowing he's locked up where he belongs."

Stan stiffened. *God, give me the strength not to hit this woman myself.*

"All due respect, but your husband just got done manhandling Buck Hayes like it was nothing. I might just have a few words of my own to describe Hap Wilkes but silly or pathetic wouldn't be one of them. Come get your husband first thing tomorrow or people around here are going to know you for what you are."

January's eyes narrowed. "And what would that be?"

Stan shook his head and smiled, not wanting to unleash his own anger and disgust upon a woman he knew more than deserved it. "Let's just say that after today I'll be sure to thank Jesus every morning I wake that you aren't my wife, January

Wilkes. And while I'm at it, I'll also suggest you be thanking God too that you have a man as patient and forgiving as Hap Wilkes."

As he began driving his car back down the Wilkes' driveway with Hap in the backseat, Stan Potts apologized to his old friend. "Sorry about that knock on your head. I was just—"

Hap nodded. "I know, Stan. You were just doing your job. Thing is I don't hardly feel this bump on my head anymore. Seems I don't feel much of anything these days . . ."

CHAPTER 17

Sheriff Potts sat at his desk staring in at the small eight-by-eight jail cell that housed Hap Wilkes. The rancher had been there for two days without a word from his wife.

The fine for disorderly conduct was forty dollars, no small sum for a poor rancher like Hap. Deputy Hayes had bellowed and moaned that Hap should be brought before the county judge for assaulting an officer, but Sheriff Potts wouldn't hear of it. There would be no formal charges, no appearance inside of a court. Things like this were to be handled with as little outside involvement as possible. It was how the sheriff had always conducted his duties and no whining deputy was going to change that.

"Buck, you really want everyone in the county to know how that man in there kicked your ass so easy? Hell, you had your gun drawn! That kind of thing gets out and guys will be lining up hoping to give you a beating. A good law man needs a reputation that keeps people in line without things getting violent, so if you want what reputation you have left shut your pie hole and let me handle Hap Wilkes."

When given that directive disguised as a warning the deputy stormed out of the Richland County Sheriff's Office but did manage to keep his mouth shut. That left Sheriff Potts wondering what was to be done about Hap and the fine his wife was clearly unwilling to pay so her husband could be released. Earlier in the day he had told Deputy Hayes to drive out to the Wilkes place and check in on January and try and convince her to pay the fine so her husband could go home.

The sheriff pulled up a chair just outside the jail cell and sat down with a just brewed cup of coffee in his hand. "Hap, you mind my asking what happened between you and January that has that woman hating you so much?"

Hap had been lying down on the narrow cot of the cell, his tattered cowboy hat pulled over his eyes. He sat up and looked at the sheriff while slowly rubbing his hands together as he considered a response. "Well, Sheriff, I think a lot of started when we had a visitor come by about a year ago wanting to buy up the ranch. He was a representative for a developer out of Helena. Said they were looking for a place to build some kind of outdoor resort for big money clients who wanted to come fishing, hunting, horseback riding, whatever. That fella offered me two-hundred-thousand-dollars, cash money."

The sheriff coughed out a portion of some just-sipped coffee. "Holy hell, Hap! Two hundred grand?"

Then it dawned on the sheriff why January was so upset. Her husband had refused the deal and January Wilkes had grown very tired of being the wife of a humble rancher with little means. "January wanted to take the money, but you wouldn't do it. Am I right?"

The rancher shrugged. "That's *my* land Sheriff. I got family buried there. What would I do with all that money? Hell, I don't want money, at least not any more than I need. I just want a place I can be left alone. A place people aren't coming around telling me what to do or say or think. It's why my family came to this country in the first place, to have a place that was *ours*, a home nobody could take from us."

Stan looked at Hap and wondered if he would have made the same choice. Around Savage, two hundred thousand dollars was a fortune and more than enough for a woman like January Wilkes to despise the man who had kept it from her.

Just then, Deputy Hayes entered and made his way to the jail cell. "Uh, Sheriff we have a situation at the Wilkes place."

Hap's eyes were wide as he stood. "What kind of situation?"

"Spit it out, Deputy," Stan said. "What's the situation?"

Buck glanced over at Hap for a second before looking back down at the sheriff. "Mrs. Wilkes is gone. The house, it's all but cleaned out. Seems she took everything with her. Pretty much all that was left was a bed, a few dirty dishes, some broken records, and that chair Mr. Wilkes threw at me the other day sitting in the middle of the living room."

Hap was quietly laughing as he mumbled several profanities under his breath.

Stan stood. "Any idea where she went?"

Hap took off his hat and stared down at it intently while turning it over slowly in his hands. "Imagine she's back at her family's place in Helena. She's been threatening to move out for months. Looks like she took my being locked up in jail as her opportunity to do so. Guess it also means she won't be paying the fine."

The sheriff's jaw noticeably tightened as he fought the urge to curse. How Hap managed to stay so calm in the face of such news was beyond him. Stan turned to his deputy and instructed him to get on the phone and confirm January's location in Helena. Then he turned back to Hap and motioned the rancher to come closer to the bars so he could whisper something to him.

"I'll waive the fine, Hap but you can't be telling anyone about it. Word gets out I didn't make you pay and I'll have all kinds of people questioning my authority, claiming I play favorites, all kinds of crap that'll have me riled up enough to shoot someone just to shut them the hell up. I don't wanna have to go there, understood?"

Hap nodded. "Understood, Sheriff—and appreciated."

Stan looked Hap up and down while shaking his head in disbelief. "Why aren't you more upset at what that woman has done to you?"

Hap appeared surprised at the question as he carefully returned the hat onto his head. "Angry? What good would that do at this point? Besides, January did like I asked. She left me my chair."

CHAPTER 18

Dog barked loudly, signaling someone was coming toward the Wilkes home.

Hap opened his eyes, trying to force out the deep fatigue that still held him in place. He could hear the faint sound of an approaching car, a sound that was somehow very familiar to him.

"Hush, Dog. I got this." He pushed himself up from the chair, pausing a moment to allow a brief bit of dizziness to pass before making his way slowly to the front window.

This isn't possible. I'm still asleep.

It was Shirley's car. Perhaps more rusted, but Hap knew it the moment he saw the old Impala. After all these years Shirley was returning to him. For the first time in a very long time, Hap Wilkes felt joy in his heart. He had dreamed of Shirley in the hospital and now by some miracle, or fate, she was coming to see him at the home they had once shared together so long ago.

As he reached out to open the front door, he could see his hands shaking, so great was his excitement. The sound of the approaching car grew louder, the engine's tone unmistakable. Even the creaking suspension was just as Hap remembered. It really was Shirley's car.

The early evening light glowed amber across the ranch property as Hap stepped out onto the front porch. He looked down and noted how dirty and rumpled his clothes were and remembered he hadn't showered or shaved in days. His face was covered in coarse, white stubble and he likely smelled every bit as bad as he looked.

Oh, to hell with it. Shirley was never one to be stuck on appearances.

Hap stepped down from the porch and began walking across the yard, his lame left leg dragging behind him. His face beamed a wide smile as he waved back and forth like an excited child greeting a best friend.

Both Connor and Sarah looked back at the impossibly happy old man shuffling toward them as they neared the small house. Sarah's face tightened with confusion. Hap Wilkes was not presenting them with the image of an intensely private and sometimes combative man described to them within Grandma Shirley's letter and by his sister, Julia.

"He sure seems happy to see us," she said.

Connor slowed the car to a near stop, having realized what was going on. He felt a stab of guilt and an even greater sense of pity. "Sarah, he thinks we're Grandma. He thinks she's come back to him. Remember, he doesn't know she was sick."

Sarah's face registered dismay at what her brother told her.

Outside, Hap continued to shuffle as quickly as he could toward the car. "Shirley! Shirley!"

The Impala came to a stop. Connor turned off the engine while Hap made his way to the driver door. Both brother and sister could hear the old man's wheezing and saw the deeply lined face covered in sweat from the effort it took him to walk outside.

Hap's smile vanished. He looked from Connor to Sarah and then took several steps backwards away from the Impala as Dog, sensing Hap's confusion, began growl.

"Who the hell are you?"

Connor was frozen behind the wheel of the car, frightened by how quickly the old man's demeanor had changed from a smiling greeting to aggressive suspicion. He looked over to the passenger seat for help from Sarah and was stunned to see she was already opening her door to step outside.

"My name is Sarah and that's my brother Connor. Are you Hap Wilkes?"

Sarah remained on the other side of the car just in case the still- growling dog decided to try to take a bite out of her. The old rancher's eyes narrowed as he stared back at the young woman who knew his name without him knowing hers.

"What do you want?"

Sarah held up the black and white photograph of Hap and Shirley Julia had given her. "Mr. Wilkes, your sister Julia gave me this picture. She said I was to show it to you when we arrived. Is it okay if I come over there and give it to you?"

Hap stood still, his eyes alternating between looking at the Impala as he fought back the wave of memories the car brought to him and then looking up at Sarah. "You spoke to Julia?"

Sarah nodded, her expression cautious, yet friendly. "Yes. Julia told me I was to give this picture to you and that you were to treat my brother and I like the family we are."

Hap's confusion became even more pronounced as his brow furrowed over the same pair of intensely focused eyes found within the much younger version of him in the photo Sarah held in her hand. "Family? What are you talking about? And where did you get this car?"

Sarah made her way slowly toward Hap as Connor opened the door and exited the Impala. Dog's growling intensified. Hap took his hand and placed it in front of the dog's nose and told him to hush.

"Please, Mr. Wilkes, look at the picture."

The rancher's hand trembled as Sarah passed the old photograph of Hap and Shirley to him. He looked down at it silently, holding the picture in his calloused hands as a faint smile crept across his face.

Hap whispered a single word, barely audible to Sarah even though she stood just a few feet from the rancher. "Shirley."

When Hap raised his head to look at Sarah his eyes were moist. "What is this about, girl? Who are you two?"

Connor moved himself next to Sarah and extended his hand in greeting, finding courage he didn't know he possessed and making sure to look the old man in eyes where he found more than a hint of his father staring back at him. "Mr. Wilkes, Shirley was our grandmother."

Hap took the young man's hand into his own, shaking it slowly, looking from Connor to Sarah, and back again. "You're Shirley's grandkids?"

Sarah smiled again as she nodded. "Yes, and you're our grandfather. Your son was our dad, Dex Beland."

Hap felt his legs go weak, making him fear he would fall to the ground. He opened his mouth to speak, but no words came out.

"Mr. Wilkes, our Grandma Shirley passed away recently. She left a letter telling us about you, the time you spent together, and wanted my sister and me to come here and meet you in person. I guess you could call it her dying wish."

Hap's mouth remained half open, his mind racing to comprehend the details of this most unexpected visit.

"Oh, I almost forgot," Sarah said. "Grandma Shirley wanted us to give this to you. It's a letter." She took out the envelope upon which her grandmother had written Hap's name.

He hesitated to accept it as an invading army of emotions crashed upon the shore of his mind. "That's from Shirley?"

Hap had asked a question for which he already knew the answer. He instantly recognized the handwriting.

"Yes," Sarah replied. "And it meant a lot to her that you have it."

Finally, Hap took the envelope from Sarah, holding both it and the photograph of him and Shirley as they sat on their horses. He stared at his name written down not so long ago by the woman he had loved and lost but had never forgotten. The faint but unmistakable scent of Chanel made its way to him, a remnant of Shirley that still clung to the paper. Hap felt hopeless, confused, and completely vulnerable, not knowing what to do next. Sarah sensed his uncertainty and placed a hand on his shoulder.

"We can go inside and give you some time to read the letter. Then, when you're ready, we can talk."

Hap nodded while continuing to stare at the envelope and the photograph. He realized that though Shirley was gone something of her, something of them, yet remained. The two young people standing in front of him were the physical manifestations of the happiest and most satisfying days of his life.

He straightened himself and cleared his throat, the familiar, self-assured determination returning. "So, your names are Connor and Sarah, huh?"

Brother and sister nodded.

"Well then, Connor and Sarah, I'm your Grandpa Hap and I'm very pleased to make your acquaintance."

CHAPTER 19

Hap appeared to be somewhat embarrassed by the sparse furnishings of the small ranch home. A single torn and tattered couch with a coffee table sat next to an even more worn chair in the center of the main living area directly in front of a wood stove. Though relatively tidy the tone of the home reflected that of its current occupant: tired, old, and broken down. The wood floors hadn't been varnished in years, the windows were covered by several layers of grime, and the smell of long-ago memories hung thick in the air.

"Don't get many visitors," Hap said. "Hell, I don't get any to tell the truth. I've never been one for entertaining. Please sit down on the couch. Can I get you some water? It comes right from the well. Best damn water in the world."

Sarah found Hap's attempts to be accommodating endearing. Though he appeared far frailer than the man in the picture Julia had given to them earlier, there still remained a sense of strength and dignity to the man even as he grunted from the effort of dragging his left leg behind him while making his way into the kitchen.

Connor was staring back at Dog, who in turn, was doing the same to him. The animal seemed increasingly fascinated by the young visitors.

When the rancher returned to the living room with two glasses of water, he noted Dog's interest. "Never seen him take to someone as quick as he seems to be doing to you, Connor. Normally, old Dog is as mean and untrusting as I am."

Dog walked up to Connor and sniffed his hand and then lay down at his feet, causing Hap to shake his head in disbelief as he placed the glasses of water on the coffee table in front of the couch. "I'll be damned. Dog's turned soft on me."

The rancher eased himself into his beloved family chair, his hands still holding onto the letter and photograph. The room went silent for several seconds.

"What happened to your leg?" Sarah asked.

"Had a stroke a couple years back that nearly killed me. Slowed me down some, that's for sure."

The uncomfortable silence returned, though, this time it was Hap who broke it. "If you don't mind my asking, can you tell me a bit about how Shirley passed?"

Connor cleared his throat. "Cancer. Took her pretty quick but she said she was grateful to have at least some time to put things in order. She kept her energy up until the last few weeks and then she kind of withdrew somewhere and never came back. She mostly slept at the very end. They had her on a lot of morphine. Russ took really good care of her."

Hap bit down on his lower lip, his already low voice going lower. "So, she didn't die alone then?"

Sarah shook her head. "No, Russ was great. He's been with Grandma for many years."

Hap gazed at the photograph in his hands. "Good to know she had someone there for her. She deserved to have someone she could count on."

Dog's instinctive nature informed him of Hap's melancholy. He rose from the floor to move himself to Hap's feet where he was rewarded with a scratch behind the ears.

"Did you know about our Dad and Mom's accident? That they were killed?"

Sarah glanced at her brother, somewhat surprised he had asked the question but also thankful he had done so. She wanted to know the answer as well.

Hap looked up at his two just-discovered grandchildren, pain and shame filling his eyes. "No, no I did not. Julia would have been the one to tell me, but she and I haven't been close for some time now."

Sarah passed the rancher the picture of her mother and father. "That's your son Dex and our mother Jessica."

Hap looked down at the image of his son as a grown man and the beautiful woman who had been his wife. The rancher's chest tightened, the hurt of the moment a great weight from which he had spent so long trying to avoid.

So much time wasted. All those years lost.

Hap sat motionless, unable to look away from the photo. He inhaled deeply and closed his eyes tight, forcing his emotions back into some semblance of order. "Was he a good man, your father?" he asked. "Did he treat your mother well?"

Both Connor and Sarah's eyes welled with tears. Connor half-laughed and half-cried a response. "Yeah, my dad was a good man. He could be tough, sometimes mean, but not once did I ever doubt he loved us more than anything. Him and Mom both, I don't think I always appreciated them like I should have."

Connor's voice was lost behind the still raw wound that was their parents' death. Sarah reached out to squeeze his hand while also looking back at the rancher and the same hazel-green eyes her father had. "They were both always there for us," she said. "*Always.*"

Hap gave her a little half-smile, his eyes pleading for the forgiveness he knew was not deserved. "Then he was a better man than me."

Sarah glanced down at the envelope still clenched in the rancher's hand. "I think it's time you read Grandma Shirley's letter, Grandpa Hap."

CHAPTER 20

Hap sat on the end of his bed staring at the envelope he knew to contain the last words Shirley would ever speak to him. A photo of his wife January glared at him from the nightstand, taken nearly twenty years ago when their marriage had settled into a pattern devoid of confrontation, but also lacking in any semblance of real love. They had become mostly silent companions, sleeping and waking together and going through the routine of daily life on the ranch. It was a life Hap knew January despised but had come to accept that any choice in the matter had come and gone.

All those years ago January had returned to the ranch and her husband, not out of love, or even jealousy, but rather simple necessity. A Helena doctor confirmed her inability to have children, and so, interest from men who might be willing to marry her should she become available, quickly dissipated. Also, when she shared with her family Hap's decision not to sell the ranch, both January's father and mother demanded she return and work on convincing the rancher to accept the offer. Even by her family's standards that was a lot of money and they wanted very much to have a daughter with access to it.

Hap had figured as much when January arrived home and demanded his affair with Shirley end and that he live up to the vows he took to be her husband until death due them part. She knew how important Hap considered a promise. A man's word was a reflection of the man himself and he had made that promise in the House of God, and so, January was right. As painful as it was for him, January's return meant his relationship with Shirley had to end.

Still, Hap didn't immediately accept Shirley's banishment from his life.

He visited the then new priest in the small Catholic Church that had served the residents of Savage for several generations. Father William Casey was nearly ten years younger than Hap, a Montana native who had devoted his life to the church and hoped to build up its presence in the vast, eastern regions of the state. He was tall, thin, with a long, narrow face and deep-set, smallish eyes that still betrayed his uncertainty in both himself and his place in the world.

The rancher met in private with the young priest and admitted his infidelity while also making the point that it was Shirley, and not January, who valued him as a man and made him happy.

Father Casey's reaction was typical of a recently ordained priest desperate to prove himself. His own life had yet to give him the kind of real-world experience that would allow greater understanding of the often complex and seemingly contradictory qualities inherent in human nature. For Father Casey there was no room for consideration of anything beyond the strict tenets of the church. He declared what Hap was doing to be a terrible sin and a betrayal against his wife.

When the rancher brought up the subject of divorce the priest scoffed, declaring the subject out of the question for any true Catholic, a response which caused Hap's temper to flare. "That's not right, Father! Me and January, we're not happy. Never really were. It was a damn mistake by two young people who didn't know any better. She left me, I found someone who respects who I am, what I am, and you're telling me that God is against that kind of happiness?"

Father Casey refused to budge on his condemnation of Hap's relationship with Shirley and the rancher's desire to end his marriage to January. "What God has joined together, let no man tear asunder, Mr. Wilkes. Most especially if that man is yourself. You spoke the vows of marriage. You made a promise, a holy declaration to your wife. Don't speak to me of happiness or understanding. That is the talk of a selfish man overtaken by the pleasures of the flesh. It is my duty to remind you of your obligation to God."

Hap glared at the priest, infuriated by the possibility of spending the remainder of his days with a woman who so clearly did not care for him. "Why should I be taking advice on love and marriage from a man who knows nothing of either one?"

Father Casey's eyes narrowed, and Hap recognized the sound of genuine anger coming from the priest. "I *do* know love, Mr. Wilkes— the love for God and His church."

"No disrespect but love for God won't keep me warm at night, Father."

The priest's mouth dropped open in shock. "Mr. Wilkes, that is sacrilege. To be so disrespectful in this House of God! We have records of your family attending this church for a great many years, a family this community deems worthy of respect as good Catholics. Why would you turn your back on that legacy by saying such things to me now?"

Now it was Hap's anger that the priest noted, as ominous thunder rolled across the rancher's eyes. "Father, don't you go telling me about my family. We were all here long before you."

"But were they here before God, Mr. Wilkes? I think not and it is to God, and them, you owe your loyalty. Every marriage has challenge. You are not the first husband to declare himself worthy of true love. What will separate you from all those others is being a man who stands on the principle of a promise—a promise to God and to your wife. Are you a man of your word, Mr. Wilkes or merely a man who breaks that word when it pleases him to do so?"

"But she left *me*, Father. January is the one who walked away from our home and our marriage."

Father Casey sensed Hap weakening. His plea for understanding was also the rancher's realization of what the priest believed he must do. "But hasn't she returned, Mr. Wilkes?"

Hap sat silent. "Yes," he eventually mumbled.

Father Casey placed his hand on the rancher's shoulder and squeezed it gently. "Then you are obligated to return to your wife and your obligations as her husband. Live up to the oath of marriage. Life cannot simply be about happiness. It must also be about honor and obligation as God intended for us. This church will not grant you a divorce. What it will do is welcome both you and your wife back to God's grace."

Hap left the church that day with both fists clenched at his side. He considered the possibility the priest was right. A man's word was his bond and the rancher had promised himself to January. She had come back and demanded that Shirley be gone. As much as it pained him to accept those terms the rancher felt himself without any other choice.

Years later after January's death the rancher took to arriving at Sunday Service just late enough that Father Casey could not help but note his arrival. Hap would then leave just early enough that the priest would see that, too. Every Sunday for the last ten years this pattern continued. Each time, Hap did so to remind the priest of his part in denying Hap the happiness he knew Shirley would have given him.

More recently, Father Casey's eyes would lock onto the rancher as he rose to leave and in that very moment Hap felt a sense of remorse from the priest. Perhaps this servant of God had developed a willingness to consider the possibility he had been wrong. Perhaps God wanted His children to find true love and know real happiness and not waste this all-too-brief moment that is life on relationships that were never meant to be.

The rancher's fingers once again traced his own name written by Shirley on the outside of the envelope, her final words to him. Once he opened it and read those words there was no hope for more to come.

There was such a terrible and painful finality to it.

Hap opened the letter.

CHAPTER 21

My Happy,

Why is it that people so often seem to wait until it's too late to remedy a wrong? In recent weeks I've been telling those around me to live life without regret. I don't say that as someone who has no regret but rather as a woman whose life has been filled with far too much of it.

I regret not telling my son of us and you. His name was Dex and he and his wife Jessica were killed in an automobile accident a few years ago. I think part of the reason I find myself so calm and accepting of my own impending death is that I've already been through the pain of losing a child, and so, having gone through that terrible thing, makes the fact of my own life coming to an end seem not so bad after all.

You would have liked your son. In many ways he was very much like you but also very different. He could be the most stubborn child, strong-willed, and yet, also willing to help out whenever he could. He grew tall and proud and met the most wonderful woman to make a family with. I think I might have resented Dex just a bit for that. He knew love and was able to keep that love, which of course, is something both you and I gave up lifetimes ago.

Looking back, I would say that your son was the best of both of us. As Dex grew older it was sometimes painful to look at him because it made me wonder what kind of man you were then and if you ever thought of me.

I have been blessed to know a man who has been both kind and supportive. We have shared many years together and I know him as the best friend I ever had. That said, if given a choice, would I have rather gone back to you again? To have found a way to make our time together work? Yes, without a doubt. Life isn't like that, though, is it? Not nearly so simple. At least it seems ours wasn't meant to be that way.

I was so angry with you when you took January back but as I grew older, less selfish, I came to understand the reasons for what you did. You were, and likely still are, a man of honor. It is one of the things that attracted me to you and ironically it was one of the things that took you from me as well. You made a vow of marriage and when your wife returned to the ranch you felt compelled to do your best to keep that vow.

That doesn't make losing you any less painful to me, just more understood. I'm sorry for the things I said, and I am even more sorry for not letting you know of your son. That is the most unforgivable thing of my life and is the primary reason I am writing to you now before it is too late.

While I can't bring Dex back, he and Jessica had two wonderful children, your grandchildren, who I hope will make the journey to see you. Connor and Sarah are both so amazing and I feel blessed to have known them better these last few years. Connor is quiet, like his dad and you, while Sarah is a bit more outgoing and adventurous, which I like to think reflects a bit of myself. And they are both kind-hearted people, and very loyal, like their mother.

If you have any feelings left in you of our time together I ask one final favor. Please spend some time with your grandkids. I promise you will be better for it. They have experienced so much loss in so few years, I think it would mean a great deal to them to discover something they did not know was there.

That something is you.

Be there for them. Teach them about who you are, your family, and the connection you have to the ranch. If you can do that you will be teaching Connor and Sarah about themselves which is something my pain and unwillingness to tell the truth to their father was not given to them by me. You can help to remedy that wrong.

I will assume that by the time you are reading this I will be gone. Who knows, though? Maybe, if true love does exist and we experienced it for that brief time long ago, perhaps I will be able to watch over you. I like to think so, but that might be the foolish girl that still lives somewhere deep inside of this old, worn-out body of mine.

No hard feelings, Hap. I mean that. I loved you and I know that you loved me. You were the most beautiful man in the world and I will always remember the best of what we had and will no longer lessen that memory by regretting what we lost.

If I'm rambling some now, I apologize. The doctors say I may not be able to read or write much longer. I can barely get things down on paper as it is. The medications tend to cloud my mind and the cancer makes me too tired to hold the pen for very long.

With whatever time you have left to yourself be a grandfather to Connor and Sarah. Do it for me and for the son you were never able to know.

With Love, and the hope of seeing you again somehow,
-Shirley

CHAPTER 22

Sheriff Dillon Potts had nearly arrived at the adult physical rehabilitation center his father Stan had been staying at since the former Richland County Sheriff broke his hip several months ago.

It seemed the longer Stan Potts remained in that facility the more he had resigned himself to simply giving up on life and letting death take him. It was that development his son found most confusing. Dillon had known his dad to be a larger than life get it done kind of man who seemed both fearless and indestructible when Dillon was growing up. Even after retiring from his position as sheriff and then watching Dillon take over, Stan Potts remained a man seemingly immune to the ravages of time.

Then came the broken hip followed soon after by a broken spirit. Whatever man Stan Potts used to be had disappeared and what remained was a tired old thing seemingly too weak to care about trying to regain his strength.

The sheriff looked down at his personal cell phone ringing where he had left it on the passenger seat of his police cruiser. The number was unknown to him. He picked it up.

"This is Sheriff Potts."

The sheriff was greeted by a very brief pause before the annoying voice of Bill Tuttle answered. "Good morning, Sheriff.

Sorry to bother you but I wanted to let you know I am sending out one of our agents to the Wilkes property to deliver a preliminary report regarding the endangered desert lizards we located on the premises. Within that report is a requirement that Mr. Wilkes not allow any use of the surrounding property by his domesticated animals. Any such animals are to remain penned at all times. This would include horses, cows, chickens, etc. If he doesn't comply, I am authorized to issue fines of up to $10,000 per offense."

The sheriff gripped the steering wheel so hard he temporarily swerved into the other lane. "Did you say $10,000, Mr. Tuttle? *Per offense?*"

The sheriff imagined the Bureau of Land Management supervisor smiling on the other end, the man's well-fed face beaming with happiness as he leveraged his power over an old, crippled rancher.

"That's correct, Sheriff. This authority is granted within the context of the Endangered Species Act. If Mr. Wilkes fails to comply with the findings report, I *will* fine him. And if he fails to pay those fines, I *will* initiate proceedings for federal seizure of that property."

The sheriff pulled into the parking area of the rehabilitation center with the cell phone still pressed to his ear. "Mr. Tuttle, you seem awful anxious to be creating some kind of conflict with Mr. Wilkes. Why the hurry to be doing this? Hap Wilkes is an old man. The only living relative that he has is a sister in another state who's probably not long for this earth either. How about you pull back a bit and leave Mr. Wilkes alone for a while?"

Tuttle's tone indicated his disregard of Dillon's request. "Don't tell me how to do my job, Sheriff."

Dillon forced himself not to open the window of his car and throw the phone onto the pavement and drive over it a few times, imagining it to be Tuttle's fat head. "All due respect, Mr. Tuttle, but you've been trying to tell me how to do *my* job since we first met. Hell, you even threatened to investigate my department."

And that's a threat I intend to keep if you attempt to prevent my office from doing its job. The Wilkes ranch is home to an endangered species. As such, it falls directly under my authority, an authority I will remind you is above your own as Richland County Sheriff."

"So, when will your report be delivered to Mr. Wilkes?"

Tuttle paused again before answering. "My agent should already be at the property by now."

Once again, the BLM agent had failed to inform the sheriff of federal actions within the county that Dillon was sworn to protect. "Is this agent armed?"

"Well, given Mr. Wilkes's willingness to threaten violence that seems only logical don't you think?"

"I tell you what, Mr. Tuttle, I'm going to end this call now before I say something less than professional. You want to keep pissing all over me and my department and the citizens of Richland County, that's your call, little man. I've worked with the feds from time to time over the years and have never experienced the level of disregard for my authority as you've shown me. So, from here on out, you go ahead and consider me a threat to whatever it is you're trying to do with the Wilkes ranch. I'll be asking some of my own questions now as well. You aren't the only one who knows people in high places, okay? If I find out you've done anything illegal, an abuse of your power against Mr. Wilkes, I'll be the first one putting my boot so far up your back end you could scratch your nose with it."

"Are you done threatening me, Sheriff?"

It was the sheriff's turn to smile. "No, Mr. Tuttle, I haven't even started. This is just a friendly chat. You'll know when I'm threatening you. Trust me on that."

Five minutes after ending his call with Tuttle, Dillon stood looking down at his sleeping father. The former Richland County sheriff appeared to have lost more weight. The skin around his face hung loosely from sharply protruding cheekbones. A mass of white, unruly hair sat atop Stan's deeply lined brow. Unlike most men, it seemed the older Stan Potts became the thicker his hair grew.

"Hey, Dad, it's me. You awake?"

Stan halfway opened one eye to glare up at his son. "Can't sleep much with people like you coming by asking me if I'm awake."

Dillon grinned and then leaned down to kiss his father on the forehead. "Glad to see you too. Hey, you want to go take a quick walk outside and get some fresh air?"

Both of Stan's eyes opened wide as he scowled at the proposal. "You know better than that. I can't hardly get up to use the bathroom let alone go for a walk outside."

That attitude was what worried Dillon so much. His father refused to push himself into any kind of real recovery from the hip injury. To Dillon it seemed the old man was already dead. Today, though, fresh from his frustrations with Bill Tuttle, Dillon refused to give up so easily.

"C'mon, Dad, you need to get moving. Your hip is almost healed, but you'd rather stay in this bed rotting away. Where's that tough guy I used to know?"

The former sheriff grunted at the current sheriff and looked away. Dillon felt the will to fight leaving him. Perhaps it was best his dad was allowed to just fade away. If a man as stubborn as Stan Potts wanted to die how likely was it anyone could change his mind?

"Okay, Dad, whatever. I give up. It's already been a hell of a morning anyways and I'm too tired to fight. Stay in bed all day, all week, who cares, right? Maybe I should just go home and get into bed myself. Be a lot easier than dealing with all this other crap."

Stan glanced at his son while shaking his head in disgust. "That ain't the kind of talk I want to hear coming from you. You're the sheriff. That means something."

Silence filled the space between father and son before Stan cleared his throat. "Trouble on the job, Sheriff Potts?"

Dillon noted how it might have been the first question his dad had asked him since his injury and he quickly answered, wanting to keep the old man's mind active on something besides his own self-pity. "Yeah, there's this thing out at the Wilkes property. The feds did some study, found endangered lizards living out there, and the guy overseeing the whole thing is a real piece of work I just want to punch in the face. More than that, they want to kill the wild horses out there. Can you believe it? Over some damned lizard."

Stan sat up in bed. "These feds are coming after Hap Wilkes?"

Dillon nodded. "Damn right they are and not being too considerate about it either. I just got off the phone with Tuttle. He's the one from the Bureau of Land Management. He already sent an armed agent out to the Wilkes place this morning to tell Hap he can't use his own land. Hap is supposed to keep his animals penned up or he could be fined $10,000 per offense."

Stan let out a low whistle. "Can't see Hap being too accommodating about that. No sir, that's gonna be one angry old Irish cowboy they'll have on their hands."

Dillon looked away for a moment, unsure if he should continue to share his concerns about the Wilkes ranch situation.

"What is it, son?" Stan asked. "Go on. Tell me what's eating at you."

Dillon looked around to make certain no-one else could overhear the conversation. "I think the feds, at least this Bill Tuttle, want that property for some reason. I don't know why, but something isn't right with how this is all being rolled out. It's like they want some kind of confrontation and I worry that Hap will be more than willing to give it to them."

The former sheriff sat quietly contemplating what his son had just told him. Dillon knew the look well. It was his dad on the job, focusing his mind on trying to figure out the angles of a case.

"Hey, instead of that walk how about we take a drive?"

Dillon tried to hide his happy shock at the request. It would be the first time his father had asked to leave the rehabilitation facility since the operation to repair his broken hip.

"A drive? Where?"

Stan slowly lowered his feet onto the floor while using both hands to push himself up off the bed and into a somewhat unsteady standing position. "Well, I haven't seen old Hap in years and think it's way past time I drop by and say hello."

A nurse was making her way toward the bed, her face a mix of stunned disbelief and genuine happiness to see her long-suffering patient attempting to get himself moving once again.

"You sure about this, Dad? You look a little wobbly."

Stan glowered at his sheriff-son. "Shut your damn pie hole and get my shirt and pants. We got work to do."

Dillon couldn't hide his smile any longer as he moved to locate his father's clothes. Hearing the old man's authoritative voice once more barking orders was like a visit from a long-ago friend who you thought you'd never see again.

Sheriff Stan Potts was back.

CHAPTER 23

Hap knew he was just dreaming, that what was happening wasn't real, but he didn't care.

Shirley was with him. They were both young and falling in love, though not yet together in that way. Hap's body was many years away from being stricken by the shackles of time and the stroke that nearly killed him.

The rancher was reliving that late-afternoon ride when he first took Shirley to the top of Vaughn's Hill. They sat on their horses moving at a casual pace and breathing deeply from the clear Montana air while enjoying the feeling of the late day sun as it neared the conclusion of its journey across the sky above them.

"This has always been my favorite part of the property. I came here as a kid to visit so I could look out all around me and pretend I was a gunslinger fighting off the bad guys."

Shirley flashed a warm smile at Hap as she imagined him as a boy. Over the last few months as the ranch had become her daytime home, the rancher's instinctive solitary nature lessened while he became more comfortable around her, sometimes talking for hours as if he was making up for all those years when he had kept his own hopes and dreams locked away safe from a world that would not understand or accept them.

Shirley understood and accepted Hap and found him to be the most beautiful man she had known, a mix of gentle strength with just a hint of vulnerability. She already yearned to spend the rest of her life with him but also knew that such thoughts were foolish since both of them were trapped in marriages that had given them little more than frustration and disappointment and despite his many appreciative glances her way, Shirley still wasn't sure Hap felt the same as she did.

On the ranch their failing marriages could be forgotten. Time stood still, and the two would-be lovers were lost in the here and now with little regard for what was to come.

Somehow Hap's consciousness allowed him to know these things within the unbound confines of his dream and he rejoiced as he slept, feeling a profound happiness he had not known since telling Shirley she must leave him.

"And you have family buried on the hill?"

Hap nodded, pointing away from the well-worn trail his horse knew as well as its own skin. "Yeah, another few hundred yards up from here. This is where we would bring them. My grandfather Vaughn said he wanted to be able to see the sun rise and set from his grave and know this was still his land. Coming from Ireland, the idea of owning your own land was very important to him. Many Irish were servants of the wealthy landlords. They lived on the land, worked it, but never had the opportunity to actually own it. That all changed for the Wilkes here. This land was *ours*."

"And is this where you'll be buried as well?"

Some might have considered the question morbid or out of character during a romantic trail ride, but Hap knew Shirley to be a commonsense sort, not shy to ask what was on her mind. It was one of the reasons he was so attracted to her.

"Yes. I'll be laid next to my family."

Hap slowed his horse and leaned over his saddle as he whispered across to Shirley. "That'll be a long time from now. There's no need to be making the arrangements just yet."

Shirley tilted her head and scowled as she attempted to look more serious. "Well, you *are* an older man, so a lady has to prepare. I worry I might just wear you out."

Hap pushed the brim of his cowboy hat up as his eyes widened. "Oh, is that right? Well, pretty lady if I had to pick a way to go out you can be damn sure that would be it."

As soon as he made the joke Hap feared it was overly suggestive but Shirley simply grinned as she moved her horse ahead of his. "Just try to keep up old man."

A short time later found the rancher and Shirley standing next to the small family cemetery looking out at the entirety of the Wilkes property. A shimmer of light could be seen to the east marking where the Yellowstone River ran along the farthest borders of the ranch.

"It really is quite a view, Hap. The kind of view that makes a person feel closer to God."

Hap put his arm around Shirley's shoulders and pulled her close. Her reaction was so similar to his own every time he stood at the top of Vaughn's Hill. The short ride there was something January couldn't be bothered with. He had long felt his wife had no interest in knowing who he really was while Shirley made it clear she wanted to know everything about him.

"It's nice to be wanted," he thought.

"Look over there."

Hap's eyes followed to where Shirley was pointing. It was the wild horses that so often crossed the Wilkes property, once again making their way toward the river. Even from the top of

Vaughn's Hill you could hear the galloping thunder as they moved across the grass-covered fields.

The look of wonderment on Shirley's face was like that of a child. "That is so amazing," she said. "They're beautiful."

Hap looked from the horses to the side of Shirley's face and back again, his heart aching with the love and desire he had for the woman who had so recently come into his otherwise routine and mundane existence. "That's freedom down there, and you're right, it's amazing. That herd was here long before my family was and if I have any say, they'll be here long after the last of us are all gone."

Shirley looked up to see Hap staring down at her, his eyes reflecting her own image back. Her body tensed when she realized that the moment she had spent the last three months hoping for was about to happen. What followed was a firm but unhurried embrace, a kiss that began slowly and then increased in both pressure and urgency as the ground beneath them vibrated from the galloping horses below.

When Hap pulled away, he appeared uncertain, even a little fearful. "I'm sorry, I—"

Shirley pulled Hap's mouth back against her own, an apology being the last thing she wished to hear from him. She held the second kiss far longer than the first, letting the rancher know that if he wanted, she would be more than willing to be his completely.

When the kiss finally ended Hap placed his hands on either side of Shirley's head and gently brushed his lips across her forehead and then moved his face down to whisper to her. "Little lady, I'm going to remember that kiss until the day I die."

Shirley nuzzled the rancher's neck and whispered back. "You better."

No words were spoken during the slow ride back to the barn. Shirley's mind was filled with the hope Hap would invite her to stay the night while he grappled with how to go about asking her.

They unsaddled their horse after putting them back in separate stables. The animals were then brushed front to back, both Hap and Shirley working more slowly than they normally would, trying to extend the moment together as long as possible without letting the other know that was what they were doing.

Eventually, though, the horses were brushed, watered, and fed. Hap stood near the barn entrance as Shirley made her way toward him.

She nearly lost hope as the two walked out of the barn and made their way toward the house, but finally she heard Hap clear his throat and then he turned around to face her.

Though looking outwardly calm, Hap was near panic as he stuck both of his hands into the back pockets of his jeans and scuffed the dirt with the toe of his boot. "So, uh, you think you might want to stay for dinner?"

Shirley said nothing as she continued walking toward the house. Nearly there, she glanced back behind her where Hap remained standing with his hands still imbedded in his pockets. He saw the familiar grin return to Shirley's face as her eyes held his, unwilling to release him.

"Just try to keep up old man."

CHAPTER 24

Connor and Sarah woke to the smell of breakfast being made. Hap was moving about the small kitchen area, scrambling several farm fresh eggs inside of the same cast iron skillet his mother had cooked on. He noted the two siblings stirring where they had fallen asleep on the living room floor.

"Best eggs in the world, fresh from the hen herself."

Connor rubbed the sleep from his eyes as Sarah rose to use the hallway bathroom. Hap nodded at Connor and then motioned for him to sit down at the handmade wooden table that sat in one of the corners of the kitchen adjacent to a window that offered a view of the porch area outside.

"You drink coffee, Connor? Got a fresh pot brewing."

"Yeah, a little cream if you have it."

Hap opened the fridge and took out a little stainless pitcher of cream and set it on the table. Connor noted how Hap seemed a bit younger and more invigorated than he had looked yesterday.

"There you go! Fresh cream the way God made it. Oh, eggs are done. Give me just a minute."

Hap shuffled back to the stove and moved a plate across the worn wooden countertop and filled a third of the plate with scrambled eggs. He then grabbed a bottle of red Tabasco and drizzled several drops over the eggs.

"Hope you don't mind a bit of heat with your eggs, but that's how we eat them here."

Connor's stomach growled in anticipation. "Sounds good, Hap. Thank you."

The rancher placed the plate in front of Connor and then sat down across from him. "Feel free to call me Grandpa if you like. Or Hap—whatever you want."

The old Mr. Coffee machine indicated the pot was done. Hap flinched slightly as he rose up from his chair and then he poured both himself and Connor a cup before sitting back down.

"So, how are those eggs treating you?"

Connor was already nearly done. "Best eggs I've ever had."

Sarah came into the kitchen. "Figures big brother is already feeding his face."

Hap got up to offer Sarah a place to sit as there were only two chairs in the kitchen. "Here you go, Sarah. Can I get you some eggs?"

Sarah sat and smiled. "Sounds good, Grandpa. I'll take a cup of that coffee too. I like it black . . . like my men."

Hap's hand froze midway between plate and pan, holding a large spoonful of eggs. He looked down at Sarah in confusion, uncertain as to what she said, or its suggested meaning, but also not wanting to embarrass Sarah by asking for clarification.

Sarah, sensing his uncertainty, shook her head while waving a hand. "An attempt at a joke—sorry."

Hap felt guilty for making Sarah feel as if she should apologize to him. "Oh, I can be a bit slow on the take sometimes, Sarah, and I don't hear so well either. No need to apologize. And hey, love is love, right? Don't matter if they're green and purple, you feel what you feel. I don't give a damn if you wanted to be with some colored boy."

Connor winced at the term "colored boy", knowing it had long ago fallen out of favor with most of society. Sarah ignored the term, though, happy to hear Hap speaking with such an open mind about relationships.

"Well thank you, Grandpa. You sound downright enlightened."

Hap grunted as he placed Sarah's eggs in front of her along with a cup of coffee. "Don't think that word has been used much to describe me. Enlightened? Not likely. Just an old boy with a bit of hard-won common sense."

"Grandpa Hap, did you read Grandma Shirley's letter last night before you went to bed?"

Hap took a deep breath. "I did. She always had a way with words. It was a very nice letter."

All three went quiet before the silence was interrupted by a series of loud, growling barks outside from Dog.

Hap peered out the window and saw a plume of dust coming toward the house as Dog's barking became even more urgent. He shook his head as he made out the dark outline of a government SUV.

"What the hell is this now?" Hap growled.

Connor and Sarah noted how quickly the rancher's demeanor changed from the relaxed and friendly man who had awoken them to the suspicious aggression that now enveloped Hap as he made his way to the front door as quickly as his lame leg would allow.

A single, uniformed park ranger emerged from the SUV. The Hispanic man was in his late thirties, tall, medium build, with a head of thick dark hair and an equally thick dark mustache that hung over a wide, slightly frowning mouth. A holstered gun was strapped to the ranger's hip.

153

"Hello, are you Mr. Wilkes?"

"Suppose I am. What do you people want from me now?"

Dog's lips pulled back to reveal his teeth while he unleashed a barrage of increasingly agitated barks. The ranger's hand moved to his weapon.

"Sir, you need to keep that dog under control, or I will."

Hap put his hand in front of Dog's nose. "Just tell me what you want."

The ranger moved slowly forward as he reached out to hand the rancher a stack of bound papers. "Mr. Wilkes, this is a copy of the findings report for your property following the recent on-site visit by BLM Supervisor Tuttle. Please review the report and then call the number in the contact section. Someone at the regional BLM office will be happy to go over any questions you might have."

Hap snatched the papers from the ranger. "I don't have a phone so guess I won't be calling. Is that it?"

The park ranger pointed at the papers in Hap's hands. "I suggest you go over that carefully, Mr. Wilkes. There are some requirements you are expected to meet, or you could face fines of up to $10,000."

The rancher's eyes widened as he began jabbing his finger in the space between himself and the ranger, each movement punctuated by a word. "GET. OFF. MY. LAND."

The ranger moved back a few feet and then once again pointed at the paperwork. "Mr. Wilkes, you are to keep any animals on the property penned at all times. They are not to be allowed access beyond the perimeter of those pens. That includes your chickens, any horses, even that dog sitting there next to you. Now I see you're upset but please remember I'm just the messenger here."

Hap began crumpling the findings report, his hands shaking in fury. "You can't tell me what to do here. This is *my* land. You hear me? My land."

The ranger looked ready to say something else but then decided against it. He returned to the SUV and drove away.

Hap was about to turn back into the home when he spotted yet another dust cloud making its way toward him. With his temper still running hot, he moved as quickly as he could inside to the bedroom as Dog followed close behind. Both Connor and Sarah watched as their grandfather began talking loudly to himself as he returned outside.

"Always taking, that's what they do. Nobody owns nothing anymore. No sir. Take-take-take. Government won't rest until it owns every bit of us."

The eyes of both siblings widened as they saw Hap holding a shotgun. Connor rose from the kitchen chair first, trying to intervene.

"Grandpa Hap, you need to calm down."

Hap was already outside standing on the porch holding the shotgun as he glared at the approaching police cruiser.

Sarah gasped as she heard the gun's booming blast rattle the kitchen window where she remained sitting. She could see a sheriff's vehicle slowing down and then stopping.

"Don't need to hear nothing from you either this morning, Sheriff. Just turn that thing around and be on your way. That first shot was in the air. The next one might not be."

Sheriff Potts got out of the car and then slammed the door. "What the hell do you think you're doing, Mr. Wilkes? I should haul your tired old ass in right now for making a threat like that. Now put that damn thing away."

155

Hap's chin jutted out defiantly. "I said turn around and get out of here, Sheriff. I won't ask you again."

"Hap Wilkes, you old stubborn son-of-a-bitch, do like my boy says and put that thing away before I shoot you myself."

Suddenly Hap saw the face of a memory looking back at him. Stan Potts shook his head and limped a few steps toward the porch.

"Is this how you greet an old friend you worthless bastard?" Stan said. "By shooting a gun off over my head?"

Hap's demeanor changed instantly, the rage in his eyes going from a wildfire to a slow burn. "Well I'll be damned. Is that really you, Stan? I heard you were laid up in the rehabilitation center after a bad fall messed you up."

The former Richland County Sheriff continued to limp his way up Hap's porch while nodding his head. "Yup, broke a hip. Heard you were having some trouble with the feds, though, so here I am. And by the way, it was my boy who told me so maybe you should thank him for that. Otherwise, I'd still be sleeping in that bed and not here to help save you from your damn stupid self."

Hap looked over at Dillon, who still appeared uncertain as to what Hap might try to do next. "So, it's your fault this pile of used up garbage is stinking up my porch now, Sheriff? Well thanks for nothing."

Stan chuckled as he extended a hand toward his boyhood friend which Hap then took into his own and shook warmly. "Nice to see you again, Hap. I mean it. I should have come out here sooner. Are you going to offer me a cup of coffee? If not, piss on you then."

Hap moved to the side to allow the former sheriff entry into his home and then motioned for Dillon to come in as well. "Yeah, you too, Sheriff. I have a fresh pot on."

Connor and Sarah were both standing between the kitchen and living room looking at the two just-arrived guests. Hap motioned toward his newly discovered grandchildren.

"Sheriff Potts, and Sheriff Potts, these two young folks here are Connor and Sarah Beland. They're my grandkids."

The mouths of both Stan and Dillon fell open as they looked at Hap and then at the two young people staring back at them.

"Who?" Stan asked.

Hap smiled at Connor and Sarah and then answered. "Shirley. Their father was . . . he was my son."

The elder Sheriff Potts moved gingerly to where Connor and Sarah stood, looking them up and down while nodding his head. "Yes, I can see the resemblance. I didn't know your grandmother Shirley well but what I did know indicated she was a quality woman. In fact, I'd say she was far too good for the likes of Hap Wilkes. It's very nice to meet the both of you."

As Connor and his sister returned the greeting, they both felt a comforting sense of welcoming. It was an odd sensation given they had never before been to the ranch on the outskirts of a sparsely populated town in eastern Montana.

It really did feel like coming home.

CHAPTER 25

Once everyone was inside the house, Hap passed the BLM findings report to Dillon who took several minutes going over it as the others waited silently. When he was finished the sheriff looked up at the others and sighed.

"I got a call earlier this morning from Bill Tuttle. He's the BLM's point man for all this nonsense they're throwing at Hap. This findings report is pretty much what he said it would be and I'll tell you right now, he isn't playing around. They'll fine you, Hap, levy the property, and then take it."

The rancher looked at both Potts men before his eyes finally locked onto the sheriff. "Are you telling me I can't even let Dog roam around my own property? The chickens? I can't ride my horse?"

Dillon frowned. "That's right."

"I don't care what those damn papers say, Sheriff. I want to know if they can really tell me I can't use my own property because I don't know what would give them that right. You're the sheriff. Aren't you supposed to be protecting *my* rights? I mean, I pay my taxes. I stay out of trouble. I just want to be left alone."

"Dillon," Stan said. "This can't be right. It just can't. I know these feds can be a real pain in the ass but to come out here and tell Hap he can't ride his horse or go for a walk with his dog? That's insane."

The former Richland County Sheriff then looked at his old friend and shook his fist in the air. "No way. I'm not letting you fight this one alone, Hap. As soon as we leave here, I'm getting a hold of everyone I know and we're calling a meeting at the grange and let them know what these feds are doing because if they can do it to you, they can do it to any of us."

"Does anyone in town know about the Endangered Species Act?" Sarah asked. "Maybe it has limitations that this guy Tuttle is keeping from you. How about contacting your county or state government?"

Stan snapped his fingers and nodded enthusiastically at Sarah. "See there. That's smart. That's how you fight back. Use their own laws against them. And I know plenty of the county government boys and there's that new congressman we just elected. What's his name? Grew up on a family farm out by Glendive, right? He seemed to be a good enough fella. I bet he'd lend us a hand with this."

The sheriff couldn't help but smile at his father's enthusiasm. He hadn't seen his dad so animated in years. "That would be Congressman Steve Moore. I endorsed his campaign last year."

"Can you contact him then? Get him to help our grandpa out?"

The sheriff looked at Connor and paused, fearing this quickly forming battle plan would do little more than poke a government hornet's nest. "I do have his contact number. We might want to slow down here just a bit though. No sense getting others involved right away if we don't need to, at least not yet."

Stan folded his arms across his chest and shook his head in disgust. "Why do you always have to play politician? You see that badge there, and that gun? You're not a politician. You're a lawman. Don't start talking that wait and see crap. It's time you let the people of this county know you are more than capable of kicking some butt on their behalf when needed."

Hap's eyes lit up at the advice of the more aggressive of the two Potts men. "That's right, Sheriff. You listen to your old man. He knows what he's talking about. People around here, we want a fighter. We want someone who will draw that line and tell these feds to go to hell. I say we kick their ass just like I kicked your dad's ass back in the day."

Stan's eyes narrowed. "Now hold on there you old pile of horse dung. I don't need to be hearing you talking up that tired story. You want to go again? I'll take that crippled leg of yours and stick it right up your ass."

Everyone waited nervously for Hap's reaction, fearing the former sheriff had gone too far and that the rancher would soon erupt in another angry outburst. The younger generation, including Sheriff Potts, didn't understand the language and mannerisms of a much tougher and more direct time when men could be throwing punches one moment and then joking about it over beers the next.

Hap broke out laughing, his head falling back and his mouth wide as he let out a series of cackles that stunned everyone around him but the former sheriff who was old enough to recall a time when Hap wasn't nearly so serious.

Stan was soon laughing as well. Tears formed at the corners of his eyes. When the laughter subsided, the former sheriff extended his hand and shook Hap's, holding the grip as he spoke.

"Swear to God, Hap, I'm going to be doing everything I can to get this sorted out for you, starting with the meeting at the grange. I'll get the word out, don't you worry. You won't be stuck out here all alone on this one."

Hap's features softened. He was genuinely touched and grateful for his old friend's support. "Thank you, Stan. I mean that."

Both Connor and Sarah watched the exchange intently, learning something of how the world once was when a man's word was their bond and support and confirmation between men was given in the form of a firm handshake.

"Okay, look, I'm not going to say you can't try to call that meeting but at the same time I don't want people getting all fired up over this. I don't want a confrontation which could lead to someone getting hurt. I'll be happy to contact the congressman and see if he has any information that might help. And Hap, there will be no more greeting visitors with a shotgun blast, you understand? Eastern Montana isn't the Wild West anymore."

Hap glowered at the sheriff and then at Stan, who held up his hands and shrugged.

"Don't look at me, Hap. He's the sheriff."

CHAPTER 26

Sheriff Potts sat alone in his office, staring down at the BLM report. Hap Wilkes was more than happy to have the sheriff take it with him, saying he had no use for the report beyond starting a fire with it. The sheriff knew Hap had been pushed to his breaking point. If the feds arrived on his land the rancher would most likely end up hurting someone or himself.

And that's exactly what this Tuttle seems to want, but why?

Maybe Congressman Moore had some answers. Dillon had known Steve Moore for the last decade. The young congressman had just started his family shortly before running for, and winning, a seat in Congress after spending eight years serving his country as an Army Ranger that included three tours in Iraq and Afghanistan.

The sheriff located the congressman's personal cell number and dialed it.

"Hello there, this is Steve."

"Yes, Congressman Moore, this is, uh, this is Richland County Sheriff Dillon Potts. How are you doing, sir?"

"I'm doing fine, Sheriff. How can I help you?"

The congressman had the just under the surface nervousness almost everyone who received a call from law enforcement found impossible to entirely overcome.

"Oh, I was just hoping to talk to you about something, Congressman. Nothing related to you. I have a situation with the Bureau of Land Management really putting the screws to one of our local ranchers. He's an old guy, barely gets around anymore, and the feds marched onto his property the other day and are basically declaring it a no use zone because of some lizards. I was curious to know if your office had any information related to that or possibly any other recent complaints against this particular BLM office?"

When the congressman replied next, all hints of nervousness were gone. "If you don't mind my asking, Sheriff, who's the rancher?"

"He's out in the Savage area—name is Hap Wilkes."

Dillon heard the congressman moving the phone to his other ear. "I know him. He helped train a horse for my mother years ago. She suffered from MS and being on a horse made her feel so much better. Mr. Wilkes donated hours of his time getting the horse ready for her. He didn't talk much, but I recall him being very up front and honest. I know my family, my mother in particular, were sure grateful for his help. It gave her a few more good years."

"That would be Mr. Wilkes, Congressman. He's about as honest as they come, but this BLM thing has him fired up and understandably so. The stress of it actually put him in the hospital just the other day."

The concern in the congressman's voice was genuine. "Is he going to be okay?"

"Well, he's already back home, but even if he wasn't okay, Hap would never let you know. He's ornery, like my dad. They must have been putting something in the water back when that generation was growing up. They all seem like such tough old coots."

"Who's the contact for the BLM office that's been involved, Sheriff?"

"That would be a Mr. Bill Tuttle and he's all in on this, I'll tell you that. He already told Mr. Wilkes he can't let his animals roam the property and that if there is a violation it could be a $10,000 fine per offense."

The congressman curse under his breath.

"Well I don't know about you, Sheriff but that sounds pretty damn outrageous. I'm going to come right out and say it. I'm not a fan of the Bureau of Land Management. I'm not a fan of most of these bloated government agencies but that particular one is right near the top of my list and it's crap like this that's the reason why. I'll be happy to make some calls on this and see if I can find out what's going on. Did I hear you right that this is about a lizard?"

"That's correct. It's apparently an endangered lizard that's been living out there for ages. Oh, and one more thing. The guy from BLM, Tuttle, he says the herd of wild horses that have been running around that area for as long as I can remember are going to be eliminated."

The congressman's tone went from controlled concern to outright shock. "They plan to kill the horses?"

Dillon was nodding to himself as he held the phone to his ear. "That's right, Congressman—every last one of them. Tuttle told me he didn't have the budget to spend on relocation."

"This Tuttle intends to kill an entire herd of wild horses for a lizard?"

Dillon continued nodding, his own disbelief mirroring that of the congressman's. "Yes sir, that's exactly what they intend to do."

"Give me twenty-fours, Sheriff. I'll be directing staff to look into this today and will get back to you on this tomorrow. You have my word."

"Thank you, Congressman. I look forward to hearing back from you tomorrow then."

At the same moment Dillon was ending his call with Congressman Moore, Bill Tuttle was having his own phone conversation with Richland County Health and Safety Commissioner, Horace McAvoy. McAvoy was born and raised in Eastern Montana and had held his position with the county for the last twenty-four years. He would be retiring in six weeks and was finally allowing himself the liberating freedom of no longer giving a damn.

"Mr. McAvoy, you received a copy of the findings report, correct?"

Horace had never met Bill Tuttle but didn't care for the man right off. Something about Tuttle's tone indicated someone yearning for more power and influence—the kind of person who had no place in government. These days, though, it seemed government was creating hordes of Bill Tuttles.

"Yes, Mr. Tuttle, I did." The health commissioner was being purposely abrupt. He didn't intend to tell Tuttle any more than was absolutely necessary.

"Why haven't you contacted me then?"

Horace extended his middle finger and directed it at the phone. "I wasn't aware I was obligated to do so, Mr. Tuttle."

The BLM agent's frustration with McAvoy's deflection was apparent as the volume of his voice rose considerably. "Mr.

McAvoy, I will assume you are aware of the influence inherent within the Bureau of Land Management. You do know you are speaking with a federal agent right now, yes?"

"Can you just get to your point, Mr. Tuttle? I'm late for lunch."

Tuttle, who sat alone in his office, shook his head in disbelief at how dismissive the county employee was of their phone conversation.

These idiots need to respect my authority.

"Mr. McAvoy, there is an unlicensed cemetery on the Wilkes ranch property. That property is also, as was clearly outlined in the report I sent you, a soon-to-be designated endangered species area. I want the remains from that unlicensed cemetery dug up and relocated ASAP."

Horace McAvoy motioned into his office the few staff who had not yet gone to lunch already and then put Tuttle on speaker phone.

"Am I to understand you want me to dig up the bodies of Mr. Wilkes' family and relocate them because you say you can't find any county approval allowing a private cemetery for his property?"

Tuttle's voice cracked from the anger he felt over being treated with such disregard by someone he deemed his lesser. "That is exactly what I want."

"Well, I tell you what, Mr. Tuttle, how about you want with one hand and crap in the other and then get back to me when you find out which one fills up first?"

Tuttle yelled into the phone. "What did you say to me?"

McAvoy looked up to see three employees of the Richland County Health and Safety Office staring back at him in amused shock. For the first time in a very long time, Horace McAvoy was thoroughly enjoying his job.

"What I meant to say, Mr. Tuttle, is that people in Richland County have been burying family members on their properties for a very long time. It doesn't happen as often today of course, but back then, which I'm pretty certain the Wilkes ranch qualifies, it was a common thing and I believe it predates any current regulations regarding private cemeteries, which by the way, *are* still allowed. So, if you want me to send a crew out to the Wilkes property to dig up some remains, it ain't gonna happen. Now good day, Mr. Tuttle, and kiss my ass."

Horace ended the call and stood up from his desk, smiling at the other Richland County employees who remained standing in stunned silence looking back at him.

"That felt damn good," he said. "Now let's go get us some lunch."

CHAPTER 27

After Sheriff Potts and his father left, Sarah asked Hap if he could show them the top of Vaughn's Hill. She wanted to look out at the property from the same view her grandmother Shirley had all those years ago.

The rancher got up slowly and lifted his arms above his head, attempting to stretch the fatigue out from his body. "I'm gonna have to ride up that way and you two can walk alongside if that's okay. I can't make that walk on foot anymore."

"That's fine, Grandpa," Connor said.

Hap looked at both his grandchildren and felt a twinge of painful regret, wishing their father, his son, could be with them as well. "I'll saddle up Peanut and we can be on our way."

"Oh, wait. What about those government papers that said the animals weren't supposed to wander around the property?"

Sarah rolled her eyes at Connor's concern. He had always been the one to follow the rules.

The rancher grunted as his eyes looked out the window and across the open expanses of the Wilkes ranch. "My land, my rules. Nobody is going to tell me otherwise."

Sarah pushed her brother toward the door. "Let's go, goodie-goodie."

It took Hap nearly an hour to saddle up. He moved slowly, stopping regularly to catch his breath. Both Connor and Sarah made over Peanut, the seventeen-year-old mare the rancher had raised since birth. She was short legged for a horse, with large and friendly dark eyes and a brown and white muzzle that would repeatedly brush up against Hap as he moved around her. The affection between horse and owner was apparent.

Once he had finally cinched the saddle firmly around Peanut's midsection, the rancher ran a work-roughened hand slowly down her short, muscular neck and told her what a good girl she was, eliciting an approving nod from the horse. "Peanut knows every inch of this property. Best trail horse I ever had. She was a sickly foal, had a rough birth, but by her second year she was proving herself to me every time we'd ride."

Brother and sister watched in amazement as Hap clicked his tongue several times while tapping Peanut's shoulder. The horse leaned down until Hap was able to comfortably place his strong right leg into the stirrup and then pull the rest of himself over and into the saddle, after which Peanut once again stood up to her full height.

"See there? That was her idea. She could tell I wasn't right after the stroke. I wasn't riding her, and she was getting anxious. Finally, one day while I was brushing her, she leaned down like that and looked back at me wondering what I was waiting for. It was her way of telling me it was time I literally get back in the saddle again. Being able to ride my property is one of the things that has kept me going these last couple years and that's all Peanut's doing."

A moment later saw Sarah and Connor walking in the tall grass alongside Hap and Peanut as they made their way slowly toward Vaughn's Hill as Dog ran happily on ahead of them.

Both of his grandchildren silently noted how Hap appeared ten years younger as he sat in the saddle, his body moving rhythmically with the motion of the horse. The rancher appeared very much to be a man at peace, despite all the surrounding pressures of ill health and the ongoing dispute with the Bureau of Land Management.

"The wood to build the home and the barn came from trees on this property. There's a stream off in that direction I learned to fish in. I bet it is still stock full of good eating cutthroat if you're interested. And over there, that clump of logs you see just poking out from the grass, that was a little fort I built when I was about ten. Used to hang out there for hours at a time pretending I was a cowboy defending the land against invading Indians. That's also where I shot my first bear."

Connor's eyes grew wide as he looked up at Hap. "You shot a bear?"

The rancher nodded. "Yup. Big old black bear that kept sniffing around the barn, ripping into the feed bags, chasing the chickens, and scaring the hell out of the horses and cows. I was twelve. My dad and I sat in that little makeshift fort and waited and waited. Hour after hour until there she came walking through the grass right toward us. I had been given an old Winchester a few months earlier for my birthday and my dad had this Marlin rifle he had ordered new out of the Sears catalog.

"Well, he aims that Marlin and it jams. The sound carried to the bear and she stands up and then charges us. Everything was in slow motion at that point, but I knew the bear was moving fast, real fast. You could hear its breath and the sound of its paws pounding against the ground.

"My dad looks down at me and says that I better hurry up and shoot. His voice was calm, but I could see the worry in his eyes.

171

Well, I take aim, hold my breath like I was taught, pull the trigger, and then move that old bolt action as fast as I can to get a new round in the chamber. It was that second shot that killed her. First bullet skimmed across the bear's shoulder but that second one hit right above the left eye. The bear went down like a sack of rocks, rolled end over end, and then lay still no more than about ten paces from where me and my dad sat inside the fort. We ate good that winter, I'll tell you that."

Sarah and Connor looked at the remnants of Hap's fort that sat some hundred yards away and tried to imagine their grandfather as a boy of twelve shooting his first bear.

"Did you tell Grandma Shirley that story?" Connor asked.

Hap smiled. "As a matter of fact, I did and it was in this very spot as I took her up to the hill for the first time, just like I'm doing with you two now."

Vaughn's Hill loomed just ahead. A scattering of trees dotted the area around its base.

"It's a short walk up to the top. Trail is easy so shouldn't be any trouble for a couple young folks like you."

It took just over twenty minutes to get up the hill. Once there, Sarah and Connor saw the family cemetery Hap had indicated to them earlier. Four graves marked the resting places of the rancher's mother and father, and grandmother and grandfather. The view from the cemetery surpassed their expectations.

Sarah imagined her grandmother looking out from the very spot she now stood, seeing the shimmering outline of the Yellowstone River to the northeast and the slowly moving green and brown grasses dancing under the push and pull of the wind that swept over the space between the hill and the Wilkes home.

It was beautiful.

Can you hear me, Grandma Shirley? I'm here where you once were. We did like you asked. We met Hap. We met our grandpa.

It wasn't the sound of Shirley's voice that answered Sarah, but rather the far off but growing closer thunder of approaching horses. The wild herd was once again returning to the ranch.

Hap pointed out toward a large dust cloud that rose up from the direction of the Yellowstone River. "There they come, making an appearance for you two just like they did for Shirley when she first made the trip up here."

Sarah could make out the outlines of several horses moving swiftly over the hard-packed earth near the river as they galloped toward the grass fields that surrounded Vaughn's Hill.

"Wow."

Connor's single word captured the moment perfectly as high-pitched whinnying cries echoed across the fields. The sound made Peanut shift nervously beneath Hap. The rancher's narrowed eyes stared down at the quickly moving wild horse herd, his face drawn tightly into a grim frown.

"Something's wrong," he said.

Both Connor and Sarah looked up at Hap and then back down to the herd, unable to tell what had him so worried.

Dog let out a low, growling bark.

"What is it, Grandpa?"

Hap told Sarah to hush as he continued to watch the panicked herd. A moment later, the air began to vibrate around them, mixing with the rumble of the galloping horses.

Connor was the first to spot it. "There, coming from the river."

A single black helicopter raced over the horses, flying just above them. Hap knew there would likely be recently born foals among the herd.

The chopper passed over the horses several more times, diving closer and closer with each pass and forcing the herd to move itself into circles, their whinnying cries soon transformed into terrified screams.

The helicopter then moved directly over Hap, Connor, and Sarah, close enough for them to make out the white-lettered Bureau of Land Management logo on both its sides. Peanut pawed the ground nervously. She wanted to bolt for home.

"It's coming back this way," Sarah cried.

Dog barked his affirmation of Sarah's warning as the chopper made a wide turn and then moved back toward the hill. Soon it was hovering no more than a hundred yards from where the three of them stood watching, before lowering slowly onto the ground.

As the turbine engine was powered down and the blades slowed, Hap watched a familiar figure emerge from the chopper. Bill Tuttle, accompanied by the same armed park ranger who had earlier delivered the findings report to Hap, had returned.

Dog, sensing the rancher's outrage and fear at the sight of the BLM supervisor, took off running toward Tuttle and the ranger, wanting to protect Hap, Connor, and Sarah from danger. Hap cried out for Dog to stop, but to no avail. The dog was running full speed toward those it deemed a threat to the humans it instinctively wanted to keep safe from danger.

"Shoot it!" Bill Tuttle screamed as he frantically scrambled to move back into the helicopter. The ranger lifted his rifle and aimed. The sound of the weapon firing cracked across the hill. Hap watched horrified as the top of Dog's skull disintegrated into a shower of blood and bone.

Sarah covered her mouth with her hands, stifling a scream while her brother stood motionless, not believing what he had just seen.

Hap sat motionless in his saddle, glaring back at Tuttle and the ranger with eyes filled by a dark and dangerous storm. His hands clenched the reins so tightly the leather cut into his skin. He knew if he had a gun, he would have shot both Tuttle and the ranger dead there and then.

The lack of a weapon did nothing to lessen his rage or desire to kill the two men. Lost in the haze of wanting revenge for Dog's death, Hap did the only thing that made sense.

He charged.

And once again the sound of Bill Tuttle's cries rang out atop Vaughn's Hill.

"Shoot him! Shoot him now!"

CHAPTER 28

The ranger lowered his rifle and shook his head. "I'm not shooting at an unarmed man, sir."

Tuttle snarled the order again as he pointed at the rancher and his horse.

"That man is a threat! If I tell you to shoot, you shoot!"

The ranger loomed over Tuttle and shook his head once again. "No, sir. That man is *not* a threat, and I'm not shooting."

Tuttle looked out across the space between himself and Hap Wilkes. Peanut, after initially moving toward the helicopter, now refused to budge, despite Hap's demands that she keep going.

"Come on, Peanut. Let's go."

The horse remained in place. Perhaps she sensed the danger to Hap in charging the chopper or possibly it was simple fear of the large flying machine, but Peanut would go no further.

Tuttle jumped down from the helicopter and motioned for the park ranger to follow. He walked as quickly as his short legs would allow until he stood directly in front of Hap and Peanut.

"Mr. Wilkes, you are in violation of the findings report. That is $10,000 per offense and I see both this horse and a dog that were allowed out onto protected property. That's $20,000 in fines you've accumulated just now. There's also the illegal cemetery. I'm reviewing that as well."

Hap remained silent, though the rancher's eyes threatened damnation upon the BLM supervisor.

"I think I'll send out a few more armed agents to your place later in the week to secure this horse. You clearly cannot be trusted to keep it penned yourself. The issue with the dog has already been resolved."

Hap winced at the mention of what had been done to Dog, but still said nothing.

"Don't you have anything to say, Mr. Wilkes?"

Hap shook his head. "Nope."

Tuttle glanced up at the armed agent and then shrugged his sloped little shoulders. "Okay, until next time, Mr. Wilkes. You know, it really is beautiful up here isn't it? And quite a nice breeze. Oh, and sorry about the dog. That thing was clearly a threat to our safety and my incident report will say just that. We had no choice but to kill it."

Tuttle paused to see if his mention of Dog's death would stir a more volatile response from Hap, but the rancher's stoic silence remained intact. Within minutes, the government helicopter powered up and rose from Vaughn's Hill to disappear beyond the borders of the Wilkes ranch, leaving Hap, Connor, and Sarah to digest what had just happened.

Peanut, sensing Hap wanted down, lowered herself closer to the ground. Soon the rancher was crouched next to Dog's body and then lifting it up against his chest. His eyes were dry and clear, any emotion over the loss of the dog pushed far beneath the surface.

"Gonna take him back home and bury him out by the barn."

Connor moved to help Hap lift Dog onto the front of the saddle atop Peanut but Sarah grasped Connor's arm and gently pulled her brother back as she whispered up to him. "He wants to do this alone."

Sarah was right. Hap grunted and strained to lift Dog's body into the saddle, his face grim, his eyes cold, and his mind filled with thoughts of revenge. He pulled himself into the saddle next, took a moment to catch his breath, and then looked down at his grandchildren.

"Okay, let's go."

Brother and sister helped dig the shallow hole behind the barn into which Dog was gently placed. Hap looked down at the remains and then closed his eyes. "Thank you both for the help."

Each of them took turns placing shovels of dirt into the grave until Dog was covered. The effort left Hap breathing heavily, his brow drenched in sweat, worrying both Connor and Sarah that he had pushed himself much too hard.

"I'm fine," Hap growled.

Sarah was still trying to comprehend the arrival of the helicopter and Dog's death. It seemed an impossible nightmare.

"Grandpa Hap, why are these people allowed to do this? I mean, they killed Dog. And I heard that man, he was yelling for the other one to shoot you. This is America, right? This kind of stuff isn't supposed to happen."

Hap placed his chin upon the end of the shovel handle and closed his eyes again. He shared Sarah's disbelief that any of this could really be happening, even as another part of him knew it was. For whatever reason known only to Bill Tuttle, the feds seemed suddenly obsessed with controlling his property.

"You know, it might be safer for you two to go back home to Arizona. It's one thing for them to shoot my dog dead but if anything were to happen to either one of you . . ."

Hap's voice trailed off as Connor shook his head. "We're not leaving you alone, Grandpa. No way. The sheriff is helping. His dad is calling that meeting. You're not alone. You have us and we're family. We stick together."

His grandson's words finally pushed down the wall behind which Hap's emotions had been hiding. The rancher's eyes glistened. It had been a very long time since Hap Wilkes had felt so loved.

I don't deserve such love. These kids, they never knew me because I was a coward. I should have fought for Shirley. Never should have listened to that priest. Things could have been different for her, for me, for all of us.

The gratitude Hap felt for Connor's demand they stay with him was overcome by the guilt he felt at not having been a part of their lives until now and even that had not been his own doing, but theirs and Shirley's.

"Hey, Grandpa, how about we get cleaned up and go for a ride in Grandma's car? Take our mind off what happened today. You can show us around Savage."

Hap smiled at Sarah, noting how beautiful his granddaughter was and how much she was like her grandmother. He shuffled next to her and placed his arm around her shoulders and squeezed her close.

"That sounds like a good idea."

CHAPTER 29

"Did I hear you correctly, Mr. Tuttle? You actually killed the man's dog?"

Tuttle was smiling to himself as he replied inside the spacious surroundings of his Bureau of Land Management office. "Yes, the creature was a threat and had to be put down. Next week we eliminate the herd. I'm moving fast on that before any kind of local opposition can be formed that might slow the intended land seizure."

"But no luck using the private cemetery against Mr. Wilkes?"

Tuttle rolled his eyes. Anthony Tyrell seemed to be a perpetual pessimist, always finding fault in Tuttle's work. "It's true the county health and safety commissioner weren't responsive, but please assure the senator and Greenex that things *are* proceeding as planned. Mr. Wilkes will be served with a $20,000 fine by tomorrow for the two violations I personally witnessed earlier today."

"And what about the sheriff? Should we be concerned about his involvement?"

Tuttle chuckled. "No, he's just a hick cop. I can bypass him and utilize BLM agents and the Montana State Patrol if need be. After we eliminate the wild horse herd my office will be monitoring the Wilkes property around the clock. It will be given top priority. The old rancher will continue to violate the terms of the findings report, accumulate fines he can't pay, and we'll seize the property from him. Simple."

Senator Mansfield's adviser paused a moment before responding. "I certainly hope so, Mr. Tuttle. Some very important people are placing a great deal of trust in your promise to make this happen."

"Well, I thank them for their trust. I only hope to be remembered when the next position becomes available in Washington D.C."

While Tuttle was working to secure his much-desired advancement within the federal bureaucracy, Sheriff Dillon Potts took a call inside of his own much smaller office from Richland County Health and Safety Commissioner, Horace McAvoy.

"Hello there, Sheriff. I hope everything's going smoothly on your end."

The sheriff hadn't spoken to McAvoy in months and couldn't recall ever taking a direct call from the health commissioner. "I'm doing fine, Commissioner. You're not placing some kind of health emergency on my desk, are you? I already have plenty of work to keep me busy."

Commissioner McAvoy cleared his throat, indicating to Dillon he was somewhat nervous. "The thing is, Sheriff, I took a call earlier from a Bill Tuttle of the Bureau of Land Management. He was asking about a family cemetery out at the Wilkes place. The man actually demanded I go out to the property and dig up the remains and relocate them."

Dillon leaned against the back of his chair while rubbing his forehead. "You have got to be kidding me."

"Wish I was, Sheriff but that's what he wanted. I figured since he's a fed, I'd better let you know. Is there some kind of trouble brewing between old Hap and the BLM?"

The sheriff looked out through the small interior window of his office and saw his dad sharing a joke with Adeline Rhodes. "Yeah, you could say that. So, what did you tell him?"

Though he couldn't see him, the sheriff sensed the health commissioner's smile on the other end of the phone. "Well, I basically told him to go to hell. Hope that was okay with you, but frankly, I'm just about ready to retire and I'll be damned if I'm going to be part of digging up some old family graves because some asshole fed tells me to."

It was Dillon's turn to smile into the phone. "I take it Mr. Tuttle didn't appreciate your response?"

"I imagine not, Sheriff, but I didn't wait around to find out. I hung up on him. I also told my staff we were not to have any further communications with him or his office until further notice. Thing is, there's something about that man's tone, something I can't quite put a finger on, that tells me he isn't right. So, if there's trouble brewing, and Hap Wilkes is on the receiving end of it could you let me know? There's a whole lot of us around here who'd like to help him out, a lot more than the old fella likely realizes."

"I appreciate that, Horace and am happy to keep you in the loop. Hopefully this thing with the BLM will blow over, but if not, I'll let you know. I appreciate the heads up."

As the sheriff ended the call, he heard the front door of the sheriff's office open and then saw Hap, Connor, and Sarah walking in. At the exact same time, his phone rang and identified the caller as Bill Tuttle.

Dillon felt yet another headache coming on.

CHAPTER 30

"Hello, Hap," Adeline said. "It's great to see you out and about. And are these your grandchildren the sheriff told me came up from Arizona for a visit?"

The rancher nodded, his face displaying his pride and pleasure at being able to tell others that he was a grandfather. Hap had spent the last hour riding inside of Shirley's old car with Connor and Sarah, showing them what little there was of Savage, Montana. He decided they should also stop to speak with the sheriff about what happened with the Bureau of Land Management, including the agency's killing of Dog.

"Yes indeed, this here is Connor and Sarah Beland. Connor and Sarah, this is Adeline Rhodes. She's actually the one who runs this place, not the sheriff."

Adeline smiled warmly as she tipped her head toward Hap. "He's right about that."

Adeline then glanced back at the rancher before her eyes settled once again on Sarah and Connor. "So, your grandmother was . . ."

"Yes," Sarah said. "Our grandmother was Shirley."

"Mr. Wilkes, Dad, can you two come into my office please?"

Dillon sensed his face betrayed more stress than he cared to show.

"Excuse us, Adeline," Hap said.

Adeline nodded. "The sheriff looks serious. Best you two get moving. I'll stay out here with Connor and Sarah."

Once Hap and Stan were inside Dillon's office, Adeline turned to the siblings and asked if she could get them something to drink.

"No thank you, Ms. Rhodes," Connor answered. "I'm fine."

Adeline waited for Connor to continue, sensing he wanted to say something more.

"Ms. Rhodes, did you know our grandmother?"

Adeline frowned as she considered saying anything more. She glanced toward the sheriff's office and then motioned for Connor and Sarah to sit down with her on the couch that served as the waiting area. Sarah found herself taken in by Adeline's warm but equally tough exterior. Though the deep lines of her face indicated her more than seventy years of age, Adeline's bright blue eyes held the light of a woman still full of energy and curiosity for the world around her.

"I guess there's no harm in my telling you what I can, which probably isn't much. I didn't know your grandmother well. We spoke a few times when she and Hap were together. I'll say this, though, I never saw Hap Wilkes so happy as when he was with Shirley. He was already known by most around here as the Irish cowboy. Actually, all the Wilkes men were called that, and Hap, well, he was a quiet, withdrawn sort—handsome, strong, but not one to say much. Certainly not one who cared for small talk.

"But around Shirley he just lit up. He would smile and joke and it was like seeing this hard shell he had built up around himself getting chipped away. I don't think anybody who saw those two together could say they didn't make the other one happier."

Adeline's voice lowered to a near whisper as she leaned closer to Connor and Sarah. "Of course, the relationship was something of a scandal. We all knew Hap and January were still married and then word got out Shirley was married as well. Tongues were wagging. But the way Hap and Shirley looked together, a lot of us assumed they'd end up married themselves, although divorce wasn't so common like it is today. Then there was Father Casey. He was just a young fella back then. I heard he really pushed Hap to take January back and that's when things must have fallen apart between him and Shirley.   One day she was here and then everyone one was saying she just up and left. I don't think Hap has forgiven Father Casey for his part in breaking him and Shirley apart."

Both Sarah and Connor sat fascinated by Adeline's telling of what she knew regarding their grandparents.

"How did the priest break Hap and Shirley up?" Sarah asked.

Adeline again glanced at the sheriff's office to make certain no one was coming. "Look, if I say anything more it would be me re-telling old gossip. I don't really know how much or little of it is actually true and it all happened such a long time ago."

"Please, Adeline," Sarah said. "I know we just met, but it really means a lot to us to learn what really happened."

"Well, I remember someone saying that while she was staying in Helena that year she was gone, January became very serious with another man. The story she told was that she left to help take care of her sick father, but we all knew better. She hated living at the ranch. As for this man January met in Helena, he was the son of a successful insurance broker. Pretty well-to-do Catholic family, the kind of family who could give her the life she wanted. The kind of life Hap would never be able to afford. I heard after January started seeing this other man that she apparently wanted a divorce. At least, that's what she was telling her friends in Helena, and her own family was apparently very supportive of the idea. They never cared for Hap, always thinking him to be too far below January's social potential.

"Then there was some kind of medical issue—not terribly serious though. Female problems of some kind that led to a doctor informing January she was not equipped to get pregnant. She would never be with child. That was the rumor anyway. Now for an Irish Catholic couple, not being able to have kids is a very big deal. When the gentleman she had been seeing learned of her condition he apparently lost interest in January and she returned to Savage a much more bitter and angry woman than when she left, which is saying something. She was intent on tearing apart any happiness Hap might have found without her. That of course meant forcing Hap to stop seeing Shirley.

"Hap didn't give in right away. He wanted a divorce from January as much as she had wanted one from him. Well, January spoke with Father Casey, begged him and the church for forgiveness, and demanded the priest help her to make Hap do what January claimed was right and honorable which was not to leave her an abandoned woman. Father Casey did just that, calling Hap in and telling him the church would never grant him a divorce from January and demanding that Hap honor the vows he made to his wife in the presence of God. For a man like Hap Wilkes, words like honor and vows really mean something. His family has always been poor, but nobody has ever accused them of going back on their word. January knew this of course and knew it was your grandfather's honor, along with the priest's help, that would force Hap back to her. And she was right. That's exactly what happened. Hap, as much as it probably destroyed him from the inside, pushed Shirley away and allowed January to return. You know, I don't think I ever saw Hap Wilkes smile after that. Not once. Well, until today that is. He clearly seems very proud of the both of you."

"That's just so sad," Sarah said. "Every time I think of all that time spent with someone you didn't love, someone who abandoned you, after having experienced real love . . . it just breaks my heart."

Adeline was now fighting back tears as she placed a hand over Sarah's. "I know, honey. Life can be very cruel and unforgiving, but I also know having you two here with him now is a real blessing to Hap. He's never had it easy but being able to see his grandchildren after all these years, there's God's mercy to be found in that and if anyone around here deserves a bit of God's mercy it's Hap Wilkes."

Adeline, Sarah, and Connor turned at the sound of the office door opening. The two Potts men emerged, their faces looking strained.

"What's wrong, Sheriff? I know that look, and it never means good news."

Dillon inhaled and then exhaled slowly before answering Adeline's question, giving his father Stan the opening to do so first.

"That son-of-a-bitch Tuttle from the BLM is issuing a $20,000 fine and levying Hap's property until it's paid in full. He told the sheriff there will be a crew out tomorrow to take away Hap's horse because he caught them going on a trail ride up Vaughn's Hill today. And that isn't even the worst of it. They killed Hap's dog. Shot it dead right in front of them."

Adeline's eyes widened in shock and then her face flushed with outrage as she stood up from the couch and pointed at the sheriff. "What do you plan to do about this? That man should be arrested. People can't go around shooting other people's dogs on their property. And they can't just show up and take a man's horse away from him. It's intolerable. We won't stand for it. None of us."

Hap's gaze drifted downward toward his boots. He seemed embarrassed to be the source of so much trouble and attention.

"This is a federal agency, Adeline," Dillon replied. "It's not that simple. I can't just go and arrest a BLM agent."

Stan turned to face his son. "Bull. You're the sheriff of this county. You can damn well arrest anyone in the county you want. I say we wait at Hap's place tomorrow for this little prick to arrive and instead of him taking Hap's horse, you arrest the bastard. Lock him up for forty-eight hours so he knows he can't just push you around like he has. We did that kind of thing all the time in my day. Hell—"

Dillon held up his hand to cut off his father's rant. "I don't want to hear about what you did in your day, Dad. This is my ass on the line here, not yours. I can't go around locking people up without justification. If I went and did that, I wouldn't be any better than the likes of Bill Tuttle."

"Yes, you would because you'd be doing it for the right reasons. You'd be doing it to protect an innocent man from being bullied by some fed psycho who's using his position in the government to try to steal my grandfather's property."

Sarah glanced up at her brother, stunned at how forcefully he was arguing on behalf of Hap. Normally she was the more outspoken one, but now it was Connor who was demanding Sheriff Potts help them. Sarah wasn't the only one noticing her brother's newfound courage either. Hap looked at his grandson with an admiring grin.

"Connor, I appreciate you wanting to protect Hap, but—"

Connor's voice drowned out the sheriff. "This isn't just about Hap, Sheriff. You seem like an honorable guy, so you already know that, right? I watched this Tuttle fly over Hap's property and chase that beautiful herd of horses like he wanted them run into the ground. And then I watched him order a dog to be killed. And after that I heard him order Hap to be shot as well. He actually wanted my grandpa dead. The man is a threat to every family in this county, yours included. In school I learned about this country's history and how sometimes it took good, brave people to stand for something or against another thing. I know that right now we're living in a moment like that and I think we would all like to think you're standing here with us. We need your help. I agree with your dad. Arrest Bill Tuttle tomorrow. Arrest him and hold him in jail for as long as you can and while he's in there get a hold of his superiors and let them know what he's doing. Make him their problem, not ours."

As Dillon stood silently contemplating Connor's words, Stan Potts extended his hand and firmly shook Connor's while looking his old friend's grandson in the eyes. "Tell you what young fella, if I still wore the badge, I'd be deputizing you on the spot right now."

Dillon cleared his throat and then sighed. "Fine, I'll be out at your place tomorrow, Hap. If Tuttle shows up to take your horse, I'll place him under arrest and hold him for forty-eight hours."

Stan clapped his son on the back. "That's my boy. I knew you'd become a real lawman yet. That'll also give me time to get the meeting at the grange together."

Adeline cocked her head as she looked at her old boss. "What meeting?"

The former sheriff crossed his arms over his chest, looking very satisfied with how things were progressing. "I'm getting the

191

word out to everyone in the area about what the feds are trying to do to Hap. I figure the more folks we have fighting for us the more chance these feds give up and leave him alone."

Adeline scowled. "You should have told me. I could help. In fact, I *will* help. When's the meeting?"

"Tomorrow evening, six o'clock."

Adeline was already moving toward her desk. "Okay, I'm on it. I'll have that grange filled to capacity. Government people going around killing dogs and taking horses. Hell no. Not on my watch."

As Hap began making his way back outside, he was stopped by the sheriff. "Mr. Wilkes, when I'm out at your place tomorrow it's my operation, you understand? You are not to be carrying a weapon or making threats. I will be the one dealing with Mr. Tuttle, not you. If you try to get involved it could be you going to jail instead of him."

Hap turned and briefly looked the sheriff up and down and then nodded as he tipped the brim of his cowboy hat. "I understand, Sheriff."

You better understand, Dillon thought to himself. *You damn well better.*

CHAPTER 31

Hap sat in his kitchen looking into the other room at Connor and Sarah who were both on the couch. The rancher was feeling tired. The day's events, including Dog's death, weighed down upon him both physically and emotionally. He had things he wished to ask of his grandchildren but wasn't sure how to go about doing so. Asking questions wasn't something Hap had done much in his life, having followed a general rule of keeping one's business their own and not prying into the lives of others.

This was different though. Time was running short and Hap needed to know. He removed the nearly full bottle of Jim Beam from under the sink, placed it on the kitchen table and then took out three glasses from the cupboard. Hap had never been much of a drinker but tonight he thought the occasion warranted something a little different.

Connor and Sarah looked up to see their grandfather shuffling toward them with the whiskey and glasses in his hands. They said nothing as he sat down and then proceeded to fill a third of each glass with the amber-colored whiskey.

Brother and sister glanced at one another, wondering what the rancher was up to. They had never had whiskey before. Between the two of them, Sarah was the one who appeared most excited by the prospect of sharing a drink with her grandfather. Hap placed his own glass to his lips and took a slow sip, allowing the whiskey to rest on his tongue for a moment before it made its slightly burning journey down his throat.

Suddenly Hap stood and moved across the room toward a dilapidated record player that sat atop a scratched and faded pine table the rancher had retrieved from the barn shortly after January had died. She had always detested the table, but Hap remembered his father making it with his own hands and when he was growing up, the table had always been the resting place for the record player from which music often played after dinner had been served.

"You two mind if I play some music?"

Connor and Sarah shook their heads as each of them sniffed the contents of their glasses. Sarah was the first to drink, followed by her brother. Both grimaced slightly at the bitter-burning taste.

Hap was making his way back to his chair when the voice of Waylon Jennings began singing of how having always been crazy kept him from going insane.

"If you don't like the taste don't worry about drinking it. In my family, when I was about your age and my folks had something serious to discuss we often did it over a glass of whiskey. I suppose these days folks would call that abuse of some kind, but we never wasted much time worrying about what others thought."

Sarah took another drink, finding the flavor a bit less repulsive than the initial taste. "Cheers, Grandpa."

The rancher smiled as he lifted his own glass and touched it against Sarah's and then Connor's. "My own grandfather would have said *slainte*. It means to your health and whether you're poor or Rockefeller, life don't mean nothing if you don't have your health. The older I get the more I understand that unbending rule of life."

Sarah took another sip and then looked at Hap. "So, if this is what your family did when discussing something important do you mind telling us what you want to talk to us about now?"

Connor had been wondering the same thing as he sat next to his sister awaiting Hap's reply. The rancher slowly swirled the contents of his glass as he struggled to ask the question. Finally, he looked up to meet Sarah's gaze, noting how similar the shape of her eyes was to Shirley's.

"I want to ask you about your father—my son. I'm hoping you can tell me more than you already have about him. I was really hoping to get a sense of who he really was. I read Shirley's version, but I would like your version too."

Sarah's mouth was stuck half open. It was now her turn to be frozen with uncertainty over what to say. Fortunately, her brother interjected, issuing a succinct response that broke the proverbial ice, allowing grandfather and grandchildren to speak openly and honestly with one another.

"Jerk."

Hap choked on his next sip of whiskey. "*What?*"

Sarah punched Connor in the shoulder. "Don't tell him that."

Connor chuckled, took a drink, and then shrugged. "It's true. Our dad could be the biggest jerk in the world sometimes. I say that out of love. Frankly, at least speaking for myself, I needed a kick in the butt growing up and he was the one who usually provided it. Mom and Dad were like yin and yang, right? They provided the balance in our home. Dad was lightning and thunder and Mom was the soft sprinkle of rain that settled after the storm."

Sarah had nearly emptied her glass from laughing at her brother's description of their dad. "I guess he's right. Dad could be a real jerk. When he was in a mood, we all ran for cover. But then other times he would surprise us and say something that cut through all the crap and made us feel completely loved and supported. My word for Dad would be complicated. Dex Beland was a complicated man."

Hap reached over to refill Connor and Sarah's glasses, feeling both pain and pride at their description of the son he had never met as Waylon Jennings sang of the Wild Ones.

"One thing I really remember about Dad is that we were expected to always, and I mean *always*, treat Mom with respect," Connor said. "If you wanted to get him angry fast, and I mean *really* angry, all you had to do was say or do something that hurt our mother. Then it was like the wrath of God coming down in our house. He was so protective of her."

Hap closed his eyes for a moment, focusing intently on his next words. "Was he a happy man, your dad?"

Sarah sensed the emotional turmoil within her grandfather. "For the most part, I think so. I'd never call Dad a cheerful kind of guy. He could be quiet, brooding sometimes, but he would laugh and joke other times. Like I said—complicated."

Connor took another sip of whiskey and then cleared his throat. "I could tell there was always a little something missing in him. A bit of blank space he wanted filled. He'd never admit that to us but as I got older, I knew that bit of emptiness was there. I think that might have been the cause for a lot of his moods. Like a toothache that never quite goes away and then sometimes flares up until it's the only thing you can think about."

Hap didn't want to ask for clarification from his grandson, but knew he must, regardless of the pain and guilt the answer would bring. He knew that guilt was his, created years earlier with long-reaching tentacles of influence upon lives other than his own, and he deserved every bit of it.

"What was the cause of your dad's emptiness, Connor?"

Both Connor and Sarah stared at their grandfather in silence for several seconds before Connor finally answered with a single word.

"You."

CHAPTER 32

Sarah woke from her makeshift bed that was Hap's living room couch to the sound of the rancher speaking with someone on the porch outside. An old wall clock indicated it was just past 7:00 a.m.

"Connor wake up. There's someone outside."

Sarah's brother had always had a knack for falling asleep anywhere he laid his head. Even the hard wood floors of Hap's home proved to be as easy a place as any for him to slumber.

"What?"

Sarah peered out the window and saw Hap talking with Sheriff Potts, the sheriff's father, and a tall, powerfully-built black man who was also wearing a sheriff's department uniform.

"It's the sheriff. He's here already."

Connor sat up and then let out a long yawn. While it was easy for him to fall asleep, waking up was another matter.

"C'mon, Connor, get up."

The front door opened as Connor got to his feet. Hap was the first to enter, followed by the three other men. The rancher then introduced his grandchildren to Deputy Bobby Houston.

"Deputy Houston, this is Connor and Sarah Beland, my grandkids visiting from Arizona."

The deputy extended a hand to introduce himself to the siblings. "Nice to meet the both of you. Sorry for all the drama going on around you right now."

Sarah looked over at Hap and issued a quick half smile. "I'm just glad to be here to help our grandpa out. Can I make a fresh pot of coffee for everyone?"

Stan closed the front door behind him and then removed his cowboy hat. "That would be very nice. Thank you."

As Sarah moved into the kitchen to make the coffee, Hap and the other men sat around the living room to discuss how to handle the possibility of Bill Tuttle's arrival and his threat to take Peanut from the ranch.

"Mr. Wilkes, Hap, I need to emphasize once again that you are not to give any indication of intended violence toward Mr. Tuttle or any other agents that he might show up here with. Do you understand?"

Hap grunted but then offered a quick shrug. "Yeah, I understand."

Dillon nodded. "Good. I've updated Deputy Houston on the situation and he is more than willing to see Tuttle arrested and held for forty-eight hours if it comes to that."

"And we are on tonight for the meeting at the grange," Stan said. Adeline told me there's going to be a great turnout. Everyone is good and pissed about what these feds are trying to do to you."

Hap nodded to his old friend but then scowled. "Good and pissed don't bring Dog back."

Sarah returned from the kitchen and placed a cup of coffee in front of each of the men. Bobby had a sip and then smiled.

"Great coffee, Sarah."

Sarah offered a quick thank you, blushing at the compliment.

Everyone in the house went quiet as they collectively looked upward toward the ceiling. A low, approaching rumble shook the home, growing louder as the air outside suddenly exploded into a tumultuous cacophony.

Two Bureau of Land Management helicopters landed nearby, some eighty feet from the barn, creating a temporary dust storm that hid the craft's occupants.

Dillon was the first to open the front door, wanting to make sure he kept himself between Tuttle and Hap. He soon saw Tuttle step out from one the helicopters. Four other armed men were emerging as well, their grim faces indicating serious business that was in no mood for opposition.

"Geez," Stan said. "They brought the whole damn hammer down on you, Hap. This is ridiculous."

Deputy Houston stood next to the sheriff and glared at the approaching BLM agents as his hand rested on top of his sidearm.

"Keep your wits about you, Bobby," Dillon whispered. "We don't need any dead or injured heroes today."

The former college linebacker's dark eyes flashed a hint of the potential fight he was itching for. "I'll follow your lead, Sheriff, but if you need me to bring the ruckus, I'm ready."

"Hello, Sheriff. I assume you are here to assist us today and help make certain Mr. Wilkes allows my men to do their job."

Dillon moved toward Tuttle as he noted the three other armed BLM agents watching him intently. "It's my understanding you think you're taking Mr. Wilkes's horse today, Mr. Tuttle. I'm curious to know how you plan on doing that with a couple of helicopters."

The BLM supervisor rolled his eyes and shook his head. "Don't talk to me like that, Sheriff. I'm not one of these dumb hicks impressed by that shiny badge on your chest. In fact, how about you look at what's coming our way right now."

Dillon looked at where Tuttle was pointing behind him. Halfway down Hap's driveway was a white government truck and matching horse trailer moving toward the ranch.

"You see, Sheriff. I'm always prepared. Now if you don't mind, we have a horse to move."

"You don't touch my horse."

Hap stood next to Deputy Houston, his eyes shooting bullets out from under the brim of his cowboy hat.

Tuttle appeared amused. "There you are Mr. Wilkes. I do apologize for what happened to your dog, but we really had no choice. We must be allowed to protect ourselves when carrying out the responsibilities we hold as agents of the federal government."

"My goodness aren't you just a steaming little pile of prissy self-importance," Stan called out.

Dillon felt the tension quickly escalating. This wasn't going the way he had hoped it would.

Tuttle tilted his head to get a better look at the former Richland County sheriff. "And who might you be?"

"He's my father," Dillon said, "and the former Richland County Sheriff."

Tuttle snorted. "One big happy family out here, huh? You people are always interesting, I'll give you that."

Bobby took a step toward Tuttle. "What do you mean by, *you people?*"

The BLM agent knew he was being baited but didn't seem to care. "I mean all of the generational inbreeding that so clearly takes place out here, Deputy. I'm more than a little disappointed to see the Sheriff hasn't yet relieved you of your duties. Don't think I've forgotten how you assaulted me the other day."

"Hell, that wasn't an assault. That was a love tap. You must really be as big of a wimp as you look."

The corner of Tuttle's lip twitched as his eyes flared in response to the deputy's insult. While the sheriff worried about yet another altercation between them his dad laughed his approval over the remark.

"One weak ass little wimp is right. Just a midget of a man hiding behind a big title. Your kind are a dime a dozen."

Tuttle turned around at the sound of the truck and trailer arriving and then smiled back at the sheriff and the others. "Laugh it up, gentlemen, but the fact remains the horse is going into that trailer and leaving this ranch *today*."

Dillon shook his head slowly as he looked directly into the BLM agent's eyes. "No, Mr. Tuttle, that's not going to happen. I'm here to protect Hap's property and I don't recognize your authority to take it."

Tuttle initially looked shocked at the sheriff's words, but that shock soon dissipated as his face broke out into a wide, cunning grin. "Sheriff Potts, are you actually willing to jeopardize your position? I assure you, that is exactly what is happening right now. I'll have your ass and badge on a plate. Do you understand?"

Bobby's face scrunched into itself, looking like he has just tasted something sour. "Is that you trying to talk tough, Tuttle? *On a plate?* What the hell does that even mean? Are you saying you want to eat the sheriff's ass? It sure sounds like that's what you're saying, but hey, I don't know, right? I'm just one of *you people*."

Dillon turned and placed a hand on Bobby's chest. "That's enough. I'll handle this, remember?"

The sheriff then turned back to Tuttle, fighting to keep his voice calm in the face of what he knew to be a quickly worsening situation. "Mr. Tuttle, I'm not allowing you to take the horse. I don't believe you have the authority to do so. Please get back into those choppers and leave."

Tuttle ignored the sheriff's words, instead snapping his fingers at the female driver of the Bureau of Land Management truck and ordering her to secure the horse that was in the barn. She was a thin woman of medium height, with reddish hair pulled back into a ponytail. Her sun-lined face suggested her age to be somewhere north of forty. She hesitated at Tuttle's directive, her eyes moving from the sheriff to Tuttle, uncertain who was in charge. Dillon recognized the woman's hesitation and quickly attempted to take advantage of it.

"Ma'am, I'm Richland County Sheriff Dillon Potts. There is a bit of a misunderstanding here. Mr. Tuttle does not have the authority to confiscate any property from this ranch. Please get back into your vehicle and leave. That's an order."

The woman looked from the sheriff to Tuttle, her expression indicating uncertainty that was quickly growing into outright panic.

"He doesn't give the orders here," Tuttle bellowed. "I do. Now go get that damn horse."

Dillon realized then how tense the BLM agents were. The distance between resolution and potential bloodshed had narrowed considerably. The woman began moving toward the barn, her eyes darting to the armed men on either side of her.

"I said you're not taking my horse." Hap had managed to move off the porch far more quickly than Dillon thought possible. The rancher was determined to put himself between the woman and the barn, armed federal agents be damned.

Those agents reacted as their training demanded, pulling their weapons and aiming them at Hap. The sheriff then heard his deputy pull his own sidearm and knew the moment was spiraling dangerously out of control. "Stand down!"

Dillon held both his hands up in front of him, his eyes pleading with the BLM agents to remain calm. "Holster your weapons, gentlemen. Bobby, you do the same. That's an order."

Stan moved Connor and Sarah back into the house, assuring them everything was going to be fine while Dillon continued trying to make certain fine was exactly how the day ended.

"Mr. Tuttle, I will ask you one more time to take your people and leave. If you refuse to do so you *will* be arrested."

"I don't think so, Sheriff. You can't do that. This is federal business. I'm the authority here, not you."

Dillon slowly moved closer to the BLM supervisor. "Please, Mr. Tuttle. We don't want anyone getting hurt. Leave now and we can discuss this situation in a more appropriate, and safer, setting."

Tuttle pointed back to the female BLM agent who stood frozen ten feet from Hap. "I told you to go get the horse. Jerry, escort her into the barn. Both of you get moving *now*."

Agent Jerry Bowls was a seventeen-year veteran of the Bureau of Land Management. The forty-seven-year-old Bowls was a man of medium height and build with a full head of brown and grey hair who appeared somewhat annoyed by Tuttle's commanding tone as he placed himself between Hap and the woman.

"Sir," he said. "I need you to move."

Hap shook his head. "No."

Tuttle moved behind the armed agent. "If he doesn't move, go ahead and place him into our custody. We can just throw him in the trailer with the damn horse."

205

Bobby took a position behind Hap, his hand once again resting on the sidearm he had just returned to its holster. "The sheriff made it clear no property is to be taken from Mr. Wilkes, his horse included. I suggest you and your agent step back, Mr. Tuttle."

Dillon moved behind Tuttle, his voice sounding far calmer and more assured than he actually was. "Mr. Tuttle, you *will* be arrested and detained. It's time for you to go."

The BLM supervisor turned to face the sheriff, pointing to the other armed federal agents who remained standing near the helicopters with their weapons pointed at Hap.

"I'm pretty sure I have you outgunned here, Sheriff. How about you shut up and let me get on with doing my job and stop this ridiculous posturing?"

Dillon leaned down to whisper to the BLM supervisor. "Mr. Tuttle, I'll say this just one last time. Leave now or you're under arrest."

"Is that right? I'd like to see you try. Your threats don't mean a damn thing to—"

Dillon locked his cuffs around Tuttle's wrists as Tuttle screamed his outrage. "What the hell do you think you're doing? Let me go."

"Gentlemen," Dillon said, "Mr. Tuttle is coming back to my station where he'll be held pending formal charges. Anyone trying to stop me from doing my duties as Sheriff of Richland County will find themselves under arrest as well. Feel free to notify your superiors of what has happened. If they have any questions, they're welcome to contact me directly."

Dillon pushed Tuttle toward his police cruiser while silently praying none of the armed agents would attempt to stop. The agents stood watching but didn't move from their positions.

By the time he closed the rear door of the cruiser to lock Tuttle in the back of the car, Sheriff Potts found Bowls standing behind him.

"Sheriff," he said. "Are you sure you want to walk this particular ledge? When D.C. gets wind of this there's going to be one hell of a political storm coming your way."

Dillon shrugged off the warning which he took as both genuine and well-intended. "You're probably right but I figure it's better than bloodshed which is what would have happened one way or the other if I let anyone take that horse away from Mr. Wilkes today."

Agent Bowls crossed his arms across his chest as he looked back at Hap. "Look, I really don't know why me and my men were sent here. Seems like a lot of unnecessary fuss, which leads me to believe someone else a lot higher up than Tuttle is pulling the levers of whatever is really going with this ranch. I will be issuing my incident report as soon as I get back to the office. I don't imagine you'll have more than a few hours after that before D.C. is directly involved, but I tell you what. When I hear what form that involvement is going to take, I'll try to give you a heads up."

Dillon shook the agent's hand as Tuttle seethed inside the back of the patrol car. He looked down at the agent's chest, noting the name on his id card. "Thank you, Agent Bowls. I appreciate that."

Ten minutes later the BLM choppers rose up and then disappeared into the Montana sky while at the same time the white truck and trailer moved down Hap's long driveway on its way back to the main road.

"So, is that it? They're giving up? It's all over?"

Connor's questions hung in the air unanswered before Dillon let out a long sigh. "I'm afraid not. This thing, whatever it might really be about, is most likely just getting started."

CHAPTER 33

The little Savage grange had never hosted such a crowd of people as gathered in the early evening following the brief stand-off at the Wilkes place earlier that morning. The low ceiling interior of the simple white building had a small plaque at its entrance indicating its capacity was forty-four. On this night, though, nearly twice that many were packed inside with nearly that number lined up outside as well.

The crowd of people was an eclectic mix of young and old farmers, ranchers, small business owners, and even a group of bikers who had rode up from Wyoming. One of those bikers was the thirty-seven-year-old nephew of Adeline Rhodes. Adeline was at the grange entrance to greet the sheriff, Hap, Connor and Sarah as they made their way through the crowd of people.

"How in the hell did so many people know about the meeting, Adeline?"

"Facebook," Adeline said with a big grin. "I'm a popular old gal."

Hap appeared nearly overcome by all the people attempting to clap him on the shoulder as he passed through them, his breathing becoming more labored as he dragged his leg behind him. Never one for crowds, the grange meeting was proving nearly as stressful to him as the recent conflicts with the Bureau of Land Management. Sarah sensed her grandfather's tension and gently squeezed his arm, reassuring him that everything was going to be okay.

As people turned to see Hap enter the building, they broke out into cheering applause, causing him to flinch, his mind unable to comprehend why so many would show up to support him. Again, Sarah was there to reassure him.

"You're not alone anymore, Grandpa and it looks like you never were."

Stan shuffled toward his son and Hap, his smile nearly as wide as Adeline's. "Can't hardly believe the turnout. Who knew old Hap was such a popular guy?"

Both Connor and Sarah began to realize Hap wasn't the only focus of attention from the those among the crowd. People were pointing and whispering at the two siblings as well. The story of Hap and Shirley had gained a new audience, told and re-told multiple times in just the last twenty-four hours. As living, breathing embodiments of that long-ago romance, Sarah and her brother had, like their grandfather, become newly anointed celebrities by the Savage locals.

Dillon strode to the slightly raised grange stage and waited for Hap and his grandchildren to take their place next to him. The crowd went quiet as it awaited their sheriff's words.

"Ladies and gentlemen, I first have to say how gratifying it is to look out at such amazing community support. I've lived in this area all my life, done my best to serve the people of Richland County, but I've never seen this kind of turnout."

"We're tired of the government telling us what to do," an older man in the back called out. "They're coming for the Irish cowboy and then one of us will be next. I say it's long overdue someone tells the feds enough is enough."

The people once again erupted into shouts and applause. Dillon located the source of the comment. Dilbert McKenna was a farmer located four miles up the road from Hap's ranch. The two men had been neighbors all their lives, and like Hap, McKenna was a widower as well, having lost his wife to congenital heart failure just last year.

Dillon held his hands up as he waited for the crowd to quiet down. "I appreciate your concern, Mr. McKenna, but the fact remains we must continue to conduct ourselves in a respectful and lawful manner. The last thing we want is to have people getting hurt. Right now, I have my deputy watching over an agent of the Bureau of Land Management. I intend to release that agent first thing tomorrow. How the feds choose to respond after that, I don't know. What I *do* know is that we can control how we respond so that nobody gets hurt because that's the last thing that any of us should want."

A wave of murmuring moved across the room and back again, the tone indicating those gathered were hoping for a far more aggressive message. Adeline stood up from her front row seat and waited to be called upon.

Dillon pointed to her. "Yes, Adeline?"

"Sheriff, it's my understanding these feds plan on slaughtering the wild horse herd that everyone here is familiar with. That herd has been around these parts for as long as any of us can remember. Do they really plan on killing them?"

Dillon nodded. "Yes."

Again, the grange erupted, forcing Dillon to raise his voice. "I can assure everyone here that I will do everything in my power to make certain that doesn't happen."

A disturbance originated from outside, followed by the large figure of Deputy Houston pushing his way through the crowd.

211

Dillon instantly noted the strained expression on his normally calm and self-assured deputy.

"You're supposed to be watching over Mr. Tuttle back at the station. What are you doing here?"

Bobby pointed at the television mounted in a corner of the grange. "You'll want to see this, Sheriff. You'll *all* want to see this. Turn on the news. They've been replaying it for the last twenty minutes."

Adeline walked the short distance to the television and reached up to turn it on, changing the channel until it showed one of the many cable news programs which currently featured someone all too familiar to those crammed inside of the grange building.

Longtime Senator Burton Mansfield's face hung over a *Breaking News* alert that continually scrolled underneath him. And underneath that image was the following headline:

"Alleged Domestic Terrorists Kidnap Federal Agent."

"Adeline," Dillon said, "can you please turn it up so we can all hear?"

Adeline raised the volume, filling the grange with the voice of Senator Mansfield.

"This kind of thing, this ongoing problem of anti-government radicals cannot be tolerated. I have already made a call directly to the governor of Montana, as well as to the White House. I want the National Guard sent to Savage and the people responsible for these actions, those who participated in the kidnapping of a man who was simply doing his job as an agent of the Bureau of Land Management, to be brought to justice. This includes the local law enforcement of Richland County, Montana, who I believe aided or perhaps are even part of this domestic terrorist group. The people of America need to know that their government will not tolerate this kind of aggression. We will never condone the actions of those who wish to harm others and every means available to our government must now be used to make this message very clear to those who would oppose us."

Dillon felt his legs go weak as the true intent of the senator's words became all too clear to him. Senator Mansfield was threatening an all-out government assault against the citizens of Savage. It was a nightmare scenario suddenly come to life.

Hap reached out to tap the sheriff's shoulder. The old rancher's face was devoid of color, his eyes a swirling mass of concern and regret.

"Sheriff, I can't have my troubles be the troubles of everyone else. I don't mind putting my own life into my own hands, but this is going too far. These people, they're good, honest, hardworking folk. They don't deserve to be a part of this mess."

Dillon began to voice his agreement when he was interrupted by someone yelling out from the back of the grange.

"I propose anyone not wanting to stand and fight for the Irish cowboy get themselves away from the area as quickly as possible, women and children in particular. As for me, I stand with God. I stand for justice. And I stand with Hap Wilkes. I'm staying here."

It had been a great many years since Father William Casey had uttered the rancher's name in public. Those old enough knew well the longstanding animosity Hap harbored toward the priest for his part in keeping Shirley and him apart.

Hap stood staring back at the priest as everyone waited to hear how he would respond. Finally, Hap offered a single nod to Father Casey and then looked out at all the others who had come to show their support for him in his fight against the BLM.

"I'm just an old man, a relic of another time. Fact is I've spent a lot of my life just trying to forget what could have been and waiting for death to come take me. I haven't had much use for life for quite some time and I'm pretty sure life felt the same about me. That all changed a couple days ago when these two young people arrived at my front door. This here is Connor and Sarah Beland and they're my grandkids. Some of you know the story behind all that and those who don't just yet, I'm sure somebody will be more than happy to get you up to speed as that kind of news has always managed to travel mighty quick around these parts."

Several of those gathered inside the grange chuckled, knowing Hap's description of how quickly gossip dressed up as news traveled in the Savage community.

"I'm not just fighting for myself here anymore," Hap continued. "I'm fighting for what kind of world is going to be left for my grandkids and their kids. You all know I speak the truth when I say this country has lost its way. Some days I don't recognize it anymore. Thing is, I blame myself for that. I blame everyone else like me who sat back and let it happen. We watched as our rights got taken away. We kept quiet about it, didn't want to be bothered, until finally, it seems we pretty much gave it all away didn't we?

"Well, no more. Not this time. They want to take my right to use my land the way I want? They think they can just come in and kill my dog and then kill an entire herd of horses because some bureaucrat says so? No sir, I'm not sitting quiet this time. I may not win but I sure as hell intend to fight."

The rancher quickly raised his hands to cut off another round of applause. "Hold up. I'm not quite done. I appreciate everyone turning out here tonight. I can't hardly believe so many of you bothered to do so, but that said, I can't ask you to do more. I don't want the possibility of someone getting hurt on my behalf. It's my problem and I'll deal with it in my own way."

The crowd went silent, confused over Hap's request that they not be involved in the fight to save his property. Adeline shook her head and then stood.

"We have family too, Hap—kids and grandkids. It's just like you said. This conflict isn't just about you, it's about *them*. It's about all of us. We're here tonight to fight. That's what this is really about—the freedom to choose. To have the final say in how you live your own life. We choose to stand with you, Hap Wilkes. This community is in this together."

Hap looked to his left and then to his right as Connor and Sarah took positions next to their grandfather, their hands grasping each of his. He had never felt so supported, so wanting to protect those he loved, and as Sarah and Connor lifted his hands upward in a show of gratitude and defiance, the person Stan Potts once called the toughest man he had ever known began to cry.

CHAPTER 34

"You're doing good."

Hap knew he was dreaming again but he didn't care. Dreaming meant a chance to see and hear Shirley as he remembered her. Dreaming meant his body was once again whole, his hands steady and strong, and his heart unburdened by so many years of regret.

"Am I, Shirl? Being around people so young, I have no idea if it's going well or not."

Shirley turned in her saddle as Hap rode alongside her, their horses ambling up to their favorite spot on the top of Vaughn's Hill.

"That's how life is, Hap. At least, that's how it should be, filled with unknowns, uncertainty, and love—lots and lots of love. Those two kids have already come to love you and I know you love them."

Hap looked out toward the setting sun and smiled. "Yeah, I suppose I do. Too bad this isn't real. Too bad what really is happening is that I'm a broken-down old man the world has no more use for. I would have liked a lot more time with Connor and Sarah and their dad and mom too, but nothing can be done about that."

Shirley scowled. "You have to stop bashing your own head into the wall of the past, Hap. There's a door in that wall. It's called the here and now and you need to open it and walk yourself on through and leave all of this self-pity behind. As tough as some people seem to think you are, I know better. Underneath the strong and silent shell, is a man hurting. You can't remake the past, but you can be a part of the future. Your grandkids *are* that future. Don't turn away from them like you did me. Don't waste what little time you have left. Make it count for something. Make it count for *them.*"

Hap felt anger well up within him. His jaw clenched as he pressed the heel of his boots against Peanut's sides, propelling the horse forward away from Shirley's stinging accusation.

"You can't run away from yourself!"

Hap jerked the reins to bring Peanut around sharply so he could face Shirley directly. "I didn't turn away from you. I never forgot. It was just how I thought it had to be at the time. I'm sorry, Shirley. I'm so damn sorry for not fighting harder but I never turned away—not completely. I would never do that."

"We both should have fought harder, Hap. I ran away from the pain of losing you and the fact is I don't think I ever stopped running. That pain never really left me. But that's okay because that's life. It's never perfect. It's never completely predictable. We just do the best we know and hope it turns out right. I don't resent you for what happened. Like you said, it was just how we thought it had to be at the time."

Hap's head dropped, momentarily hiding his face from Shirley's view. When it rose up slowly from underneath the wide brim of his hat, the Irish cowboy stared back at the love that should have been. Shirley held his gaze as tightly as she knew she should have held onto him those many years ago.

Hap finally tore down the wall inside of him and felt decades of self-imposed regret let loose. Shirley was right. A person was a fool to keep living in a past that could never be changed.

There was only the here and the now.

To hell with former mistakes.

To hell with might-have-beens.

And even though he knew this was a dream, a trick of the mind, Hap decided it was time he stopped living to die and instead started dying to live.

The Irish cowboy dropped smoothly from the saddle and walked with slow purpose toward Shirley and her horse. He looked up at her with the slightly crooked smile that had ensnared her from the moment she first saw him.

Shirley tensed as Hap's hands suddenly reach up for her. He grasped her under her arms and then easily lifted her down from the saddle. It was a gesture that reminded her of his great strength that came from years of hard work. Where other men obsessed over appearance and their physicality, the rancher's power was simply the result of who he was and how he lived. He wore that strength as naturally and comfortably as other men might a pair of comfortable shoes.

Hap looked down at Shirley, his eyes taking in every detail of her face, lovingly tracing the outline of her eyes, nose, cheeks, lips, and chin. His rough hands gently held the back of her head as he moved himself closer.

The gentleness of Hap's hands contradicted the aggressive passion of his lips. From the moment their mouths touched, the kiss was as much an act of near violence as it was one of love.

Shirley welcomed that violence, wanted that violence, and returned it with an ample serving of her own. She sensed Hap's initial surprise at her aggressive response, followed soon by his approval. He matched Shirley's lust and then quickly surpassed it as his fingers worked through her hair while his mouth remained an extension of hers.

Once the kiss finally ended, Hap and Shirley stood silently holding one another as the setting sun cast long shadows across the expanse of the Wilkes property.

"I swear to you, Shirl, I may not be able to do anything about it now, but if somehow we get to be together in another life, I'm never letting you go—not ever."

Hap felt Shirley rest her head against his chest as he inhaled the familiar scent of her Chanel. He wondered, even though he knew this to be a dream, if it might somehow also be real.

Real or not, the Irish cowboy was grateful for the moment, knowing that it, like all other things in life, would not last. He cradled Shirley's hand into his own and began to dance. Unlike that time in a Glendive bar some forty years earlier, it was Shirley who now quietly hummed the words of that same Waylon Jennings' song to Hap as the ever-present gentle breeze of Vaughn's Hill enveloped them both.

I'm for law and order, the way that it should be.
This song is about the night they spent protecting you from me...

Chapter 35

"Congressman Moore do you mind telling me what the hell you think you're doing asking these kinds of questions? I for one don't like getting a blindside phone call from senate staff telling me a member of my caucus is stirring up things they have no business stirring up. At the very least you should have afforded me the courtesy of a heads up. You just got elected to Congress for God's sake. This is not the kind of fight you start picking at this juncture of your political career. At least not if you hope to be re-elected."

House Majority Leader Rayford Farrington sat behind the large desk of his large office in the confines of the Capitol Building glaring back at the junior congressman from Montana. Moore had received an early morning phone message from Farrington's office demanding he stop in to meet with Congressman Farrington personally.

The demand from a member of his party leadership wasn't unexpected. Congressman Moore had spent all of yesterday asking questions from various committee chairs regarding why the Bureau of Land Management was making such a strong play for the Wilkes property. He met with one stonewall response after another. The day ended with a call to the Secretary of the

Interior, a woman by the name of Tamara Jackson who had been nominated to the position by the President of the United States.

The congressman suspected it was that call and brief conversation with Secretary Jackson that resulted in his being called onto the proverbial carpet by House Majority Leader Farrington.

"Sir, I represent the interests of the citizens living in my district, not the feelings or suspicions of other politicians making their living in Washington D.C. I have reason to believe a federal agency is abusing its powers at the detriment of a rancher who wants nothing more than to be left alone. I'm looking into the possibility of that abuse, nothing more."

Congressman Farrington was fifty-three, spoke in a somewhat high-pitched Boston accent, and yearned to be the next Speaker of the House. He had been a member of Congress for nineteen years and knew well the signs of a newly initiated member of government who had not yet balanced idealism with common-sense and political survival.

"Congressman Moore, I do appreciate you wanting to help the voters who granted you the privilege to represent them. That said, if you persist in these inquiries, I will have no choice but to reassign you to scrubbing toilets in the House gym. If you have a question, if you want to contact a member of the administration, you contact this office first. You understand?"

Moore knew Farrington's type well. He was like some of the military officers he had served under. Men and women who had not seen one minute of battle but thought themselves superior to those who had. They were in the business of self-promotion and would attempt to destroy anyone, or anything, deemed a threat to that end. The newly-elected congressman looked back at the bald, shiny dome of Congressman Farrington and shook his head.

"I'm sorry, sir, but that isn't going to happen. I didn't swear an oath to the House chain of command here. I swore to uphold the Constitution and what's going on at that ranch back in Montana is a violation of a man's basic rights to privacy and property. I want answers and I intend to get them."

Congressman Farrington stood up, revealing his middle-aged paunch not quite hidden under the blue silk tie that accompanied his dark suit. "You will do as you're told, Congressman. I'm telling you this for your own good, your own *protection*. I didn't get to this office by chasing every wrongdoing I thought might be happening against somebody. You need to the see the bigger picture. You're not good to your district if you aren't allowed to have any say around this place, and without a decent committee assignment you might as well not show up at all."

Congressman Moore remained unimpressed by the Majority Leader's implied threats. "I don't believe anyone needs to sit on a committee in order to stand up for the truth."

Farrington pointed at Moore. "Don't be an idiot. You won't last around here if you keep this holier-than-thou crap up. You know that, right?"

Moore could see Farrington's eyes narrowing from behind the thick glasses he wore over a large, wide nose. The tip of the nose was reddened by a disjointed map of broken capillaries, likely the result of years of hard drinking. He stood and then looked down at the much shorter and older Majority Leader.

"It seems we're done here, Congressman. I intend to continue looking into this situation with every resource at my disposal, including contacts back in Montana. In fact, I will be calling the governor as soon as we're finished here. I'm also considering sending inquiries to a number of media sources."

Farrington sat back down and motioned for Congressman Moore to do the same. "Okay, look, this Montana ranch deal is something of a pet project for some influential people around here. I don't know the particulars. I just know you've managed in a very short amount of time to piss them off. I have a duty as House Majority Leader to protect the party. This thing you're doing could create the kind of blowback we want to avoid."

Congressman Moore, who had already sat down again, leaned forward in his chair, sensing he was about to receive at least some of the truth regarding what was really going on with the Wilkes property. "What senate office contacted you? You started our meeting saying you didn't like being blindsided by a call from senate staff. So, who's the senator involved in this?"

Farrington leaned back in his chair at the same time Congressman Moore was leaning forward. The Majority Leader glanced toward the door of his office to make certain it was still closed.

"You familiar with the saying, *catch a tiger by the tail?*"

Moore shrugged. "Yeah, sure."

"Well, that is *exactly* what you're doing with these questions. You're in danger of catching a tiger. It's going to turn on you and rip you down the middle before you know what's happened. My advice is for you to let it go and move on. That'll be better for you and better for the party."

Moore felt his temper stirring within him. The talk of protecting political leverage above all else was sickening. "I'm not interested in the party or my political career. What I *am* interested in is doing right by an old Montana rancher who is getting pushed around in a way I can't ignore. If you weren't such a pile of self-serving crap you wouldn't ignore it either because if this government can do it to him, it can do it to any of us."

Farrington clapped slowly as he smiled back at his party colleague. "GREAT speech, Congressman. In a few years you'll have to learn how to fake that kind of moral passion. If you do, you just might be president someday."

Moore sat waiting for the Majority Leader's turn at mocking him to end. When Farrington realized he would be unable to push him away from his search for truth involving the Wilkes property, he stopped clapping and held his hands up in front of him.

"Okay, I give up. You want to terminate your time here in D.C., go ahead. I'll have party leadership notified within the hour that you are not to be trusted—with *anything*. You can forget GOP funding for your next campaign because we'll be funding someone else. In fact, I'd suggest you not run for re-election, Congressman because we are going to primary the hell out of you. It might be best if you just fade on out, no fuss, no muss. Now get the hell out of my office."

The former Army Ranger turned congressman stood and extended his hand, appearing nothing more than bored by Farrington's refusal to assist in finding out what was going on with the BLM's sudden obsession with the Wilkes ranch. The House Majority Leader was temporarily surprised by the gesture but found his own hand reaching out as a matter of habit. After nineteen years in Washington D.C., shaking hands was an integral part of Rayford Farrington's DNA.

Once Congressman Farrington's hand was firmly in his own, Moore pulled him violently toward him while grabbing onto the congressman's tie with his other hand and wrapping it around the Majority Leader's neck. Moore then pulled the end of the tie upward until Farrington's face began turning various shades of red and purple as pools of spit dripped out of the corners of his mouth.

"I asked you a question, Congressman Farrington. Who is the senator involved in the Wilkes property?"

Moore felt Farrington already growing weaker. The man talked a good fight but was physically incapable of actually putting up much of one. "Mansfield," he croaked.

"Very good," Moore said. "Now I'd like to know who's behind the senator's interest in the property. And don't pretend you don't know. You look into my eyes. That's it, you keep looking. I'll snap your neck in this office if you lie to me. Don't test me. Just tell the truth."

To reinforce the threat, Moore pulled up on the tie an inch further, bringing Congressman Farrington to the brink of passing out as the silk fabric cut into his flesh.

"Greenex," he gasped.

Moore let go of the Majority Leader's tie. Farrington fell back into his chair, his eyes wide with fear and rage. Moore counted on there being more fear than rage, which would keep the Majority Leader from crying out for help.

"Thank you for the information, Congressman. I really do appreciate your cooperation. And since you just told me something *you* know, I'm happy to share something *I* know. Regarding the good-looking little lady you have working reception in the hall outside this office, I know all about what you've been doing with her. And while I'm not entirely sure how your wife feels about her husband nailing a twenty-something staffer, I do know the media would have a field day with it. In fact, I'm pretty sure any chance of you becoming Speaker would be all but finished. I'm not one to gossip, though. You have my word on that so long as you manage to keep your mouth shut regarding the discussion we just had."

As the Majority Leader watched the Montana congressman casually make his way out of the office, Farrington realized just how much he had underestimated him.

Congressman Moore was likely to do just fine in D.C.

CHAPTER 36

Despite the troubles involving his ranch and the feds, it was Sunday morning and for Hap Wilkes that meant it was time for church. He had not missed a morning service for decades, though, on this particular Sunday, for the first time since Father Casey had demanded Hap honor his vows of marriage to January and denounce his love for Shirley decades earlier, he entered the service on time and absent his normally focused resentment toward the priest. Father Casey had voiced his support for the rancher during the previous night's meeting and it was a gesture that had meant a great deal to Hap, a sign that long-standing animosities should at long last be forgiven.

Connor drove Hap and Sarah to the church in Shirley's car. The small parking lot was already nearly filled to capacity as families who had not attended service for some time, or were not even Catholic, were making their way inside. It appeared the rancher's ongoing conflict with the feds had reignited Savage's deep sense of community.

When Father Casey looked out at the overflowing numbers of family and friends packing the twelve rows of handmade pews inside the small Catholic church, his ruddy face beamed back at them with pride. Following last night's community meeting the priest had suspected a larger than normal crowd for morning service, and so had spent several hours preparing the sermon. While he had given countless such sermons over the years, Father Casey found himself feeling nervous, uncertain that he was up to the task of delivering the kind of message the moment deserved and that the people of Savage needed to hear. He stood behind his podium and cleared his throat, noting how both his hands trembled slightly as he glanced down at his notes.

"I am going to dispense with the normal rituals of our Sunday service today. We have many with us now who are not Catholic, but who have simply come to show their support for Hap Wilkes and his fight against the federal government. In recognition of that, I wish to simply speak to you as God's servant and a friend to this community. My many years here have allowed me the great blessing of coming to know most who call this place home. It has been my honor to do so and on this morning, I stand before all of you humbled and grateful that so many are here now in God's Holy Church.

"This wonderful community came together last night as well, answering the call in a way rarely seen in this time of seemingly never-ending self importance."

Even as he read from his notes, part of Father Casey's consciousness drifted back to the time when both he and Hap Wilkes were much younger men and the rancher hoped to secure release from his vows to January—a release the priest would not grant him.

In the years that followed his admonition against Hap and his yearning to know real love, Father Casey grew ashamed at how dismissive he had been of the situation. Youth and idealistic fervor were rarely a productive or capable combination and the priest knew his role as spiritual adviser had been hampered by that very condition the day Hap came to him for help.

What the priest did not know is that after leaving that all too brief meeting with him, Hap Wilkes returned to his truck parked outside the church where January sat waiting, her eyes instantly betraying her sense of triumph in knowing her husband had not been given the release from marriage he hoped Father Casey would grant him.

After Hap took his place behind the wheel, January turned her head to look at the rancher as one would when scolding a puppy. "Had enough of this foolishness, Hap? Good. Then it's time to go home."

Hap drove his pickup until he came to the stop sign at the intersection of Lewis and Clark road. He knew Shirley was waiting for him at the bar in Glendive. She had pleaded with Hap to meet her there, but also made clear that if he didn't show she would know Hap had chosen to remain with January.

Seconds turned to minutes as the truck sat idling at the intersection, the rancher's heart torn between turning left and making his way back to Shirley or turning right to drive back to the ranch and accept the obligation and burden of a loveless marriage. January sat motionless, her eyes looking calmly through the windshield, sensing the great crisis being waged within the husband she despised and confident of the choice he would ultimately make.

Hap's hands gripped and re-gripped the steering wheel. His eyes shut as he recalled the many horse rides he and Shirley had shared and her laugh, her temper, and the adoration she openly felt for him. It's a rare and wonderful thing to have a woman who makes a man feel like a man and Shirley had given Hap that gift.

The rancher's jaw clenched as he recalled the words of the priest.

You are obligated to return to your wife, Mr. Wilkes. Live up to your obligations as husband. Live up to the oath of marriage. Life cannot simply be about happiness. It must be about honor, and obligation, as God intended for us.

Hap turned right. January smirked. She had won.

Husband and wife returned to the ranch where each of them settled into the life-draining routine of no longer living, but merely existing. That existence continued year after year until finally cancer brought January's own private suffering to an abbreviated conclusion while leaving Hap with the long-ago memories of what might have been had he turned left instead of right at that intersection all those years ago.

A great rumble from outside shook the interior of the church, interrupting the priest's sermon as all eyes rose upward toward the ceiling.

A low-flying helicopter passed over the church on its way to the Wilkes ranch, followed by another helicopter doing the same.

Father Casey held up his hands, hoping he didn't appear as panicked as he felt. "Everyone please remain calm."

Sheriff Potts stood up from his pew at the same time his cell phone began ringing. He too asked that those inside the church remain seated. "Just sit tight, everyone. Let me find out what's going on."

Dillon moved quickly toward the back of the church while holding the phone to his ear, having recognized the number as that of Congressman Moore.

"Yes, Congressman, what can I do for you?"

"Sheriff Potts, my office just found out there's a whole slew of feds coming your way. They intend to eliminate the herd today."

Dillon moved just outside the church entrance, hoping his voice wouldn't carry back inside. "We just had a couple choppers fly over town. Looks like they're heading toward the property right now."

"Sheriff, I've found out who the two big players are in this move against Mr. Wilkes. One is Senator Mansfield and the other is a company called Greenex that just happens to be a big political donor to the senator and several others here in D.C. There's a thirty-million-dollar windmill project already approved for a portion of the Wilkes ranch, a place the locals around there apparently know as Vaughn's Hill. I wish I had found this out sooner, but my office just confirmed it all this morning."

The sheriff peered down the street, thinking he heard something coming toward him. "Mansfield? Hell, I voted for that snake. Guess that explains his public comment about how Mr. Wilkes and my department are domestic terrorists. So, he's got his hands all over this government windmill project, huh? How's that even legal?"

Congressman Moore grunted. "From what my office has uncovered so far there's no evidence the senator has any direct ties to Greenex so proving he's abusing his power in fast-tracking the project would be difficult. And even if it *was* proven, he'd probably just get a slap on the wrist from the Senate Ethics Committee. They all do this kind of crap around here. It's just a matter of the few that get caught from time to time."

The approaching noise grew louder. It was the unmistakable sound of a large diesel-powered engine. "Look, Congressman, I have an entire community fired up about what's being done to Mr. Wilkes. They find out the feds have shown up out there today . . . I don't know if I can keep this thing contained. People are going to get hurt."

"I'm doing all I can from here, Sheriff. I already have a call into the governor's office, State Patrol, anyone I think might be able to help you and Mr. Wilkes out."

Dillon turned to see the large metallic grill of a military transport vehicle rumbling down the rural streets of Savage, Montana.

What is this, some kind of invasion?

The sheriff heard the church doors opening behind him as several people moved outside to see the source of the noise. The transport vehicle drove slowly past the church as the stern faces of no fewer than a dozen Homeland Security officers carrying military grade assault rifles stared back at the citizens of Savage.

"My God, son, it's an invasion."

Dillon turned to see his dad staring at the transport vehicle as it rumbled by, his eyes wide as his head shook slowly in fearful amazement.

"Sheriff, are you still there?"

"Yeah, Congressman, I'm here. A dozen armed federal agents just passed by me in a military transport truck. Looks like Homeland Security."

Dillon heard another phone ringing from wherever the congressman was calling him from. "I have another call, Sheriff. It might be the governor. You hold tight and keep those people safe while I keep working to get this shut down on my end. Don't know if I'll be able to make that happen in time to save the horses, though."

Dillon glanced at Hap and his grandchildren as they emerged from the church. The rancher's narrowed eyes and clenched fists indicated he already knew what was likely happening.

"I know, Congressman. Just do your best. I'll be in touch."

Dillon moved toward Hap as he attempted to make his way back to the parking lot.

"Out of my way, Sheriff. I'm no fool. I know where those choppers are headed. They're going to kill the horses, aren't they? Just like that little prick Tuttle said they would."

Stan moved next to his son and placed a hand on his arm. "You can't let them get away with this, son. We're all here for Hap. We're all ready to fight."

A crowd gathered quickly behind the former Richland County sheriff, their murmurs growing louder and more agitated.

"Everyone, please listen," Dillon shouted. "Those were armed federal agents that just drove by. If we go out to Hap's place waving guns at them then we look just like the domestic terrorists they say we are and that will give them the authority to defend themselves. People could die. I can't allow that to happen. I'm ordering you all to stay in town. Do you understand? That's an order."

Father Casey made his way toward the sheriff until he stood directly in front of him. "When justice is done, it is a joy to the righteous but terror to evildoers."

"I'm sorry, Father. What are you talking about?"

The priest looked past the sheriff at all the others who had attended the morning prayer. "It's Proverbs 21:15, Sheriff. I won't tell you how to do your job anymore than I would expect you to tell me how to do mine. I do believe, though, that part of your purpose with this community is to bring joy to the righteous and fear to those who would do them wrong. Hap Wilkes is being wronged and we are looking to you to help us fight it."

Hap, with Connor and Sarah standing next to him, held up his hands and waited for the crowd to grow quiet. "I'm going back to my property to see if anything can be done to save the horses. I

235

don't expect anyone else to do the same. Seeing you all at the meeting last night and now here again this morning is more than enough. The sheriff is right. We can't have people shooting at one another."

As Hap turned to make his way back to the Impala, Deputy Houston's patrol car sped down the street and then came to a screeching halt in front of the church. Bobby emerged from the vehicle looking stressed.

"Sheriff, I was heading back to the station and saw at least four feds standing guard at the entrance. They were armed to the teeth. I turned around before they saw me. Looks like this mess just got real."

Despite his deputy having just told him so, Dillon still found it hard to believe what was happening was actually happening. If this kept up the entire county would be under government lock-down.

"Son," Stan said. "This begins and ends at Hap's ranch. That's where you belong. That's where we all belong. We make our stand there against these people. Enough is enough. I'm heading out there with or without you and I imagine most here intend to do the same."

Dillon knew his dad was right. He couldn't control everyone. Not without doing to them the very thing the feds were attempting to do to Hap—take away his freedom at gunpoint.

"Okay, we go to the ranch, but we do it *my* way, understand? I'll lead. The rest of you follow. That includes you, Hap."

Stan grinned and gave Dillon a wink. "Atta boy."

Hap nodded his agreement and stepped aside to allow Dillon to be the one to lead them back to his ranch. Even as he did so, though, a cold shot of foreboding passed through him.

Something wasn't right.

CHAPTER 37

Sarah glanced over at her grandfather while she drove the Impala behind the sheriff's patrol car. She sensed his nervousness.

"Everything is going to be okay, Grandpa," she said. "You have a lot of people supporting you."

Behind the Impala were a dozen more cars and trucks from people who had left the church to join Hap's fight to protect the wild horse herd from the feds. Before leaving the church parking lot, Adeline promised many more were already on their way as well.

Just don't let anyone get hurt today. Not on my behalf.

As Hap silently voiced that thought, Sheriff Potts was taking another call from Congressman Moore. "Go ahead, Congressman."

"Sheriff, I spoke personally with the governor. He's sending a state patrol unit out to the ranch to help keep things calm, but it won't arrive for another hour or so. Sorry I can't do more right now. I left a message with the Secretary of the Interior but so far, no response has come back to my office. I'll keep at it though."

Dillon shook his head. A single state patrol unit wasn't likely to do much to help control over a dozen Homeland Security officers and Bill Tuttle.

"Thank you, Congressman, but unless you can get someone to tell these feds to stand the hell down, I'm worried there's going to be some kind of conflict and it's going to be messy."

"I know, Sheriff. The governor assured me they're looking into it. He was surprised as I was that all of this was going down like it is. I'm going to push that he orders some Montana National Guard units to head out your way."

Dillon calculated the closest National Guard base to be at least a four-hour drive from Savage. "I'd appreciate that, Congressman, but until then we're going to be on our own. I'll be doing my best to keep everyone calm and alive until the cavalry arrives."

Dillon ended the call and glanced over at his father.

"You're right," Stan said to him. "We're on our own out here—always have been. I'm proud of you, son. You driving out to Hap's ranch is you being the sheriff for all these people driving behind us. That's the obligation they entrusted you with and you're doing right by them, That makes me a very proud father. You might just end up being a better sheriff than I ever was."

Stan Potts had never been a man to give copious amounts of praise to anyone or anything. In fact, Dillon couldn't recall ever hearing him ever being so supportive of him. "Thanks, Dad. Just do me a favor and be careful today, okay?"

The elder Potts shrugged off his son's concern. "Bah! A couple days ago I was rotting away in a rehabilitation center bed. Now I'm on the job with you. I'm done with being careful. It's good to finally feel alive again."

When Dillon turned onto the Wilkes ranch, he looked up through the patrol car windshield to follow the path of one of the government helicopters as it sped toward Vaughn's Hill. He drove toward Hap's home slowly, locating the military transport vehicle parked outside the barn. Two armed men ran out from inside the barn, yelling at one another, though the sheriff was unable to hear what they were saying.

Both of the Homeland Security officers stopped when they saw the sheriff's patrol car and then pointed their weapons directly at it.

"Look at them treating the sheriff of this county like you were Taliban or something. It's disgusting."

Dillon agreed with his father's outrage. These feds were well beyond out of line. "Stay in the car, Dad."

The sheriff emerged slowly from his vehicle and then closed the driver door, all the while keeping his eyes on the two Homeland Security agents. "You two mind lowering your weapons? My name is Sheriff Dillon Potts. We have a whole lot of people making their way here and it's my job to make sure nobody gets hurt."

Each of the armed agents was no older than thirty. They looked nervous, which in turn made the sheriff nervous. Armed and on the brink of panic was never a good combination.

A horrific, shrieking cry sounded from inside the barn. The two agents glanced at each other and then looked past the sheriff at something behind him.

"Sir, don't move!"

Dillon turned to see Hap shuffling toward the barn, his mouth twisted into a feral snarl as he glared at the feds. "You don't be telling me where I go and don't go on my own damn property! What did you do to my horse?"

The sheriff realized then the source of the shrieking cry. It was the sound of a horse in terrible pain.

Yet another cry issued from the barn, causing both agents to wince. The taller of the two answered Hap by first shaking his head in confusion.

"Sir, we were ordered to secure any animals in the barn for transport. The horse, it fought, and somehow it rose up and fell back against the wall and I think . . . I think maybe it broke something. We tried to see what was wrong, but it won't let us near it."

Hap continued walking into the barn, ignoring the rifles pointed at him. Dillon moved his hand to the top of his still holstered side arm.

"That man has every right to check on his horse, gentlemen. I suggest you let him get to it."

A crowd had gathered behind the sheriff's vehicle. Adeline stood alongside Stan, who had ignored his son's orders to stay in the car. Next to Stan were Connor and Sarah. Behind them were nearly forty others from the church who had already arrived at the ranch, including Father Casey, who emerged from the group and then stood next to Dillon.

Peanut screamed again.

"Sheriff, I need you to come in here *right now!*"

It was Hap, yelling from inside the barn, his voice cracking, overcome with emotion.

Dillon stared at the two federal agents, waiting for them to give their approval for him to enter the barn. The taller one nodded once while looking past the sheriff.

"Just him," he said. "The rest of you stay put."

The gathering of Savage residents murmured their disapproval but did as they were told while Dillon moved quickly to see what Hap wanted. Peanut lay her side with her head somehow twisted underneath one of her front legs. Her eyes rolled wildly inside of her head as Hap whispered softly to her while running his hand slowly down her back.

"It's going to be okay. It's going to be okay."

Hap was lying. Peanut was already well on her way to dying. Her neck was fractured in the space between ears and mane. She had panicked when the armed men attempted to remove her from the barn, reared up and then fell backwards with the full weight of her body, ripping apart the top portion of vertebrae. The injury had not entirely severed the horse's spine, though, thus allowing her to feel every bit of the pain from the terrible trauma.

Despite that pain, Peanut's trust of Hap was enough to calm her. She no longer struggled to regain her feet, instead focusing on Hap's soothing tone and the feel of his hand gently stroking her body.

Rancher and horse had known one another for nearly eighteen years. Hap had raised her almost from birth and over the years, Peanut provided him the ability to temporarily transport himself away from the monotony of a loveless marriage as she and the rancher rode across the open, untamed expanses of eastern Montana.

Dillon stood still, looking down at Hap and then realizing the rancher was quietly sobbing. The old man's shoulders shuddered from the effort to keep those sobs from being heard.

Without looking behind him, Hap extended a trembling hand toward the sheriff. His voice was a gruff, pained whisper. "Need your gun, Sheriff. I can't have her suffering like this."

Dillon opened his mouth to deny the request and then abruptly closed it. He reached down and removed the gun from its holster and then gently placed it into Hap's hand.

The rancher's sobs subsided as he took the gun while also slowly tracing the upper portion of Peanut's forehead with the fingers of his other hand. The horse's breathing was increasingly labored as her back legs began to jerk uncontrollably.

Hap leaned over and kissed Peanut just behind her ear, the place she had always enjoyed being scratched when Hap brushed her after a long ride. He leaned toward the front of the horse and inhaled deeply as he looked into Peanut's large eyes. She had calmed considerably, though, he knew the pain remained as intense as before. She groaned and then closed her eyes.

Peanut was letting Hap know that she was ready.

Hap raised the sheriff's gun until it rested against the upper middle portion of Peanut's forehead. He located the mark his fingers had just traced, the area that would ensure a quick and painless death for his longtime riding companion.

Peanut's back legs trembled again as a low whining sound issued from deep within her chest.

The sound of the gunshot reverberated inside the barn, causing Dillon's ears to ring.

Hap's aim proved true.

Peanut's suffering was ended.

And then another gunshot was heard, this time from outside the barn.

CHAPTER 38

"Hap, give me my weapon!"

The rancher rose up from Peanut's body slowly with the sheriff's gun still in his hand. The sound of angry shouting from outside filled the barn's interior.

Hap looked down at the gun and then stared at Dillon. There was a pause before he gave the sheriff his weapon. Hap looked shrunken, weak, and lost. For the first time in his life there seemed to be no fight left in him.

With his gun returned to him, Dillon turned and ran outside. His father lay on the ground clutching a bloodied right shoulder while the two panicked Homeland Security agents pointed their weapons at the crowd of Savage residents and ordered them to get back.

"Sons-of-bitches shot Stan!" Adeline was livid, pointing back at the two feds, her eyes livid while showing no fear of the weapons pointed back at her.

"I'm going to need you two to lay down those weapons," Dillon said. "You've just shot an unarmed man."

The taller of the two agents glanced at the sheriff who stood just ten paces away pointing his gun at them. His face was drenched in sweat. The gunfire from inside the barn had startled the agent and when Stan moved forward to see what was happening in the barn the agent shot him.

"I told everyone to stay put, Sheriff. He didn't obey orders. He was moving in an aggressive manner."

Dillon took two very slow and deliberate steps toward the Homeland Security officers with his trigger finger ready to fire at the slightest provocation. "That man is a former law enforcement officer and also happens to be my father."

Stan was helped to his feet and then positioned himself between his son and the two federal agents. "I'm fine, Dillon. Got a nice chunk taken out of my shoulder and as soon as my adrenaline shuts down it's gonna hurt like hell, but I'm okay."

The agents appeared genuinely relieved to hear that the bullet wound wasn't serious.

"Good," Dillon said, "but these two are still laying down their weapons. I'll be damned if I let them point them at us anymore."

The shorter of the two Homeland Security agents shook his head and raised the assault rifle until it pointed directly at the sheriff's chest. "Sir, that's not going to happen. You need to step away and join the others."

"The sheriff said to lay down your weapons! Now do it!"

Deputy Bobby Houston had silently made his way behind the feds with his gun aimed at them. Stan grinned while tipping his head in the direction of the deputy.

"Now that's a good lawman right there. If I were you two, I'd go ahead and put those rifles of yours down on the ground. You've already shot an unarmed old man. I'd say you've done more than enough for one day."

With both Sheriff Potts and his deputy surrounding them front and back, the two agents leaned down and placed the assault rifles at their feet. The taller agent scowled back at the sheriff while in the distance, a BLM helicopter flew over Vaughn's Hill. Bobby moved quickly to take the agents' handguns from them as well.

"Now what, Sheriff?" the taller Homeland Security agent asked. "There's a dozen more of us securing the hill up there and we have two more choppers locating the horse herd. You're still outgunned."

Tuttle's voice crackled over the agents' two-way personal radio devices. "This is Agent Tuttle. We've located the herd. My vehicle is stuck on the other side of the ravine. I'm going to make my way to the top of the hill where I want Chopper One to pick me up after the herd has been eliminated. We should have this wrapped up within the hour."

Hap, who had stood motionless and silent since emerging from the barn, suddenly lifted his head to glower at the agents. "Tuttle is going to be up on the hill, huh?"

Hap whirled around and began shuffling toward Vaughn's Hill. Suddenly, he fell, his mouth hitting the compacted dirt and gravel that surrounded the barn. He cried out in rage.

Connor and Sarah ran to their grandfather's side to help him up, but Hap shouted to be left alone, knocking their hands away. "I'm no cripple! I don't need you two coming here and stirring up things that were better left forgotten. Just go home, the both of you. Go home and forget all of this. Go home and leave me be."

Connor backed away from Hap, stunned and hurt.

Sarah didn't move, though. Instead, she stared back into the eyes of the man who had once loved her grandmother. She refused Hap's demand to be left alone. He wouldn't get away with that. Not this time.

"No, Hap, we're not going anywhere. You can't keep running away from who you are because *we* are who you are. You can't run away from us any more than we can run away from you."

Sarah put her hands under Hap's arm to lift him up, but he pushed her away, his tear-reddened eyes flashing dangerously at his granddaughter while his hand rose. Sarah attempted to scramble backwards as she realized he intended to strike her.

That intent never found its mark, though, as Connor's hand clamped around Hap's wrist and held it firm. The rancher struggled against his grandson's grip, but then realized he lacked the strength to break free. Connor was too strong.

"I won't let anyone hurt my sister, Grandpa. Not you, not anyone."

A rush of terrible shame washed over Hap as he saw the fear that still remained in Sarah's eyes—fear of him. He knew it was his own guilt, his own pain, his own resentment of all that life had taken from him, that turned him into the monster who had just threatened physical harm against his own flesh and blood.

"Sarah, I am so sorry."

Connor released Hap's wrist and allowed him to move toward Sarah and take her into his arms where he held her tightly against his chest. Sarah hesitated for a moment and then hugged her grandfather even more tightly, her tears wetting the front of his shirt.

"Can you forgive me, Sarah? Can you forgive an angry, stupid old man?"

Sarah leaned back to wipe her eyes and then she shook her head. "It's not about *me* forgiving *you,* Hap. It's about you forgiving yourself. That's what Grandma Shirley wanted. She wants you to let it go. All of it—just let it go."

Dillon stood behind Hap and cleared his throat, waiting to get the rancher's attention. Hap turned, no longer bothering to try to hide his tears from the sheriff or anyone else.

"Mr. Wilkes, you want to head on up the hill with me? If that's where Tuttle is going that's where I intend to be waiting for him."

"What do you plan to do to him?" Hap asked.

Dillon looked toward Vaughn's Hill, watching as another helicopter circled the ranch above them. This helicopter wasn't from the Bureau of Land Management, though. It was a news helicopter from the local TV station in Helena.

The sheriff knew that likely meant Congressman Moore alerted the media and at least some of that media had already arrived on the scene. That would exponentially increase the heartburn of those responsible for initiating the abusive actions against the Wilkes ranch, particularly Bill Tuttle and the BLM.

"I'm going to arrest Tuttle and I was hoping you'd be standing there with me when I did. I figure we can take back Vaughn's Hill together."

Hap straightened his shoulders and adjusted his cowboy hat as a trace of a smile cut across the deep crevices of his face.

"I'd like that, Sheriff. I'd like it a lot. Let's go get the bastard."

CHAPTER 39

The journey up Vaughn's Hill was done using the military transport truck left by the Homeland Security agents beside Hap's barn. Nearly everyone from Savage who had arrived at the ranch to support Hap indicated they wanted to make the trip to the top of the hill as well.

Initially, Dillon balked at so many coming with them, but repeated prodding from his dad finally changed his mind. He scolded the elder Potts for not getting himself to the hospital, but Stan shrugged off the shoulder injury as nothing serious. Confirming the gash in his father's shoulder was no longer bleeding much, Dillon loaded up the truck and started driving.

Hap pointed through the windshield toward the hill. "This won't get us all the way up. Trail is too narrow. We'll have to walk the rest."

Dillon slowly made his way across the open field, following the horse trail created by years of rides from the barn to Vaughn's Hill. "Well, I figure halfway up is better than not, Hap. Are you okay to walk the rest?"

Hap didn't respond right away. His eyes locked onto the hill that had been a symbol of his family's journey to America and the subsequent sweat and toil of their life on the ranch. It had been a hard life, but up until recently, one lived on land that was theirs to do with as they pleased.

"Yeah," he murmured.

Dillon knew the old rancher was struggling to keep his emotions under control following the death of his horse. He also knew the trip to the top of the hill might provide a temporary distraction to make that struggle just a bit easier on him.

In the back of the transport truck, Stan began to sing the *Battle Hymn of the Republic*. Dillon initially rolled his eyes at the exaggerated expression on his father's face as he leaned toward the two cuffed federal agents and yelled out the first verse:

"Mine eyes have seen the glory of the coming of the Lord!

He is trampling out the vintage where the grapes of wrath are stored!

He hath loosed the fateful lightning of His terrible swift sword!

His truth is marching on!"

Stan then stood up, clapped his hands together, and demanded that everyone sing along with him. Dillon was about to yell for his dad to sit back down but seeing him looking so much like the man he had been before age and injury had, until a few days earlier, confined him to a rehabilitation center bed waiting to die, caused him to pause. As bad as Stan's singing was, Dillon loved hearing his father's voice shouting with defiance across the open fields of the Wilkes ranch, and soon, Stan had everyone in the transport truck, including Hap himself, singing along as well.

"Glory, glory, hallelujah!

Glory, glory, hallelujah!

Glory, glory, hallelujah!

Our God is marching on!

"In the beauty of the lilies, Christ was born across the sea! With a glory in his bosom, that transfigures you and me! As he died to make men holy, let us live to make men free! While God is marching on!

"Glory, glory, hallelujah!

Glory, glory, hallelujah!

Glory, glory, hallelujah!

Our God is marching on!"

The trail up to Vaughn's Hill narrowed just as Hap said it would, requiring Dillon to slow the truck's progress and then finally stop it altogether. It would be another two-hundred yards to reach the top.

As the people of Savage began helping one another to exit the back of the transport vehicle Dillon saw two more armed federal agents walking down the trail toward them. He addressed the Savage citizens, making certain his voice remained calm.

"I am to do the talking here. We don't want any conflict with these men. Deputy Houston, free the agents from the handcuffs."

The deputy paused as his eyebrows arched. "You sure about that, Sheriff?

Dillon nodded. "Yeah and hurry up."

Once the two feds were freed Dillon instructed them to follow him as he made his way toward the other two feds.

"Stop," one of them shouted. "Don't move."

Dillon did as he was told. He carefully watched as the two other agents, their assault rifles pointed at him, walked toward him and the others.

"I'm Richland County Sheriff, Dillon Potts. I'm here with the owner of the property and some members of the community who are also here to monitor what you're doing. I've been in direct contact with Congressman Steve Moore and I believe the local media is flying one of their choppers above us as well."

One of the two armed agents stepped forward and looked Dillon up and down. He had wide, dark eyes within a clean-shaved, square-jawed face. "We know who you are, Sheriff. As for that media chopper, we've already ordered it out of the area. It'll be gone in a minute or two. I don't care about some congressman. My men and I are here on very specific orders. I'm going to ask you to get the hell off this hill."

Dillon's phone began ringing. It was Congressman Moore.

"Good timing, Congressman. I'm at the Wilkes ranch having a discussion with a Homeland Security agent at this very moment."

"Sheriff, there's someone I would like to introduce you to, and if some of Tuttle's men are there, all the better. Put me on speaker please."

The sheriff raised the volume of his phone as loud as it would go and then waited, holding the phone in front of him to ensure as many people could hear whoever it was the congressman seemed so eager to introduce them to.

"Is this Sheriff Potts?"

The gruff voice was unfamiliar to Dillon. "Yes sir. Who is this?"

"Sheriff, this is Major General Kyle Radford, commander of the Montana National Guard and State Director of Military Affairs. I have been instructed by the Governor of Montana to intercede on behalf of a Mr. Hap Wilkes. Am I to understand there are Homeland Security agents with you?"

Dillon glanced up at the feds who stood staring at him. "That's correct, General Radford."

Both BLM helicopters were making their way toward Vaughn's Hill.

"And do any of those agents want to admit to being in charge of the mess going on out there?" the general asked.

Dillon looked to the feds for a response. The square-jawed agent who had directed the sheriff and the others to vacate the hill cleared his throat as he looked nervously at the phone.

"This is a Bureau of Land Management operation, sir. My men are simply here to provide assistance."

The Major General's voice exploded from the cell phone. "Who am I speaking to? Give me your name."

The Homeland Security agent cleared his throat again. "Uh, I'm Agent Mike Pensky, sir. I wish to emphasize again that this isn't a Homeland Security operation. The man in charge is Bureau of Land Management supervisor, Bill Tuttle."

"Okay, Agent Pensky, I'm ordering your men off the Wilkes property immediately. That directive comes from the governor himself, so I suggest in the strongest terms that you start moving your ass."

Agent Pensky looked at the other three federal agents who stood next to him. Their eyes indicated they would like nothing more than to terminate this operation and be done with it. Still, Agent Pensky was familiar with basic protocol and didn't believe Major General Radford had the authority to dictate orders to him or his men.

"All due respect, sir, but I'm a federal agent. I don't answer to you or the governor."

Sheriff Potts and Agent Pensky as well as everyone else standing next to them, looked up toward the sound of a single F-15 fighter jet scorching through the sky as it sped by like an impossibly fast, metallic bird of prey no more than two hundred yards over their heads. After the fighter plane nosed upward to disappear into the clouds, the sound of Major General Radford's voice again bellowed from the sheriff's cell phone.

"You hear that, Agent Pensky? That's the sound of my boot getting ready to plant itself deep into your backside! I have three more F-15s on their way and an entire artillery unit scheduled to arrive within the hour. Perhaps you don't fully appreciate the gravity of the situation you now find yourself in. There will be a thorough investigation of whatever mess is going on out there and who do you think is going get pinned with the blame once that investigation is concluded? You think it's going to be any higher ups or is it more likely to be some poor little Homeland Security grunt who thought he was just providing *assistance* to the Bureau of Land Management? Last chance, son. Shut it down and get out of there. You leave now you'll probably end up with a commendation. Stick around and they are going to drag you and your men through the mud on this and leave you holding the blame bag."

Agent Pensky looked at his men and then stared at the sheriff's phone as the F-15 began another run toward Vaughn's Hill. Even before the agent spoke Dillon knew the man's resolve had crumbled.

"Get the men down from this hill. We're out of here. Sheriff Potts, this operation is officially being handed over to you. Good luck dealing with Tuttle."

The residents of Savage erupted in applause. Hap said nothing while his eyes remained fixated on the top of the hill where he knew Tuttle would soon be arriving. He grimaced as he moved past the Homeland Security agents and began shuffling himself up the narrow horse trail. He had no intention of letting Tuttle come down the hill alive. He owed a terrible debt and Hap intended to see that debt paid in blood.

CHAPTER 40

"Look at that pathetic fool."

Stan Potts gleefully pointed down toward the ravine that ran along the north side of Vaughn's Hill. Tuttle was scrambling across the broken rocks and loose dirt that made up much of the ravine's surface. Another BLM agent, a man clearly younger and in much better condition than Tuttle, had to repeatedly stop and wait for his short-legged and profusely sweating counterpart to catch up.

The Homeland Security agents had already left the ranch. Before departing, Agent Pensky informed the sheriff it was Tuttle's intention to wait for whatever remained of the horse herd to be pushed his way by the choppers and then shoot them down as they neared the base of the hill. Tuttle's vehicle had become stuck, though, and so now he intended to make his way to the top of the hill where a BLM helicopter would pick him up.

"Look there, the choppers."

It was Father Casey who pointed a finger up at two distant black dots that steadily grew larger in the partly cloudy, late-morning Montana sky.

Dillon put a pair of binoculars up to his eyes and confirmed Father Casey was right. The two BLM choppers were making

257

their way back to Vaughn's Hill. The media helicopter had already left the area, having been ordered to do so by Agent Pensky.

"You have a sharp pair of eyes, Father. I don't see the herd though. Maybe they managed to get away."

Dillon felt Hap's eyes on him. The rancher knew the chances of the herd surviving Tuttle's intentions unscathed were slim to none. The use of helicopters would make certain of that.

A strong gust of wind blew across the top of Vaughn's Hill at the very moment Hap whispered three words. "There they are."

Hap knew exactly where to look to mark the herd's arrival. Horses, like people, were creatures of habit. Once they had established a pattern, they tended to keep to it.

The horses were running toward the ravine as they always did when passing by Vaughn's Hill. This time, though the pace was unusually fast as the confused and panicked animals attempted to outrun the helicopters flying above them.

Hap heard gunfire and then saw one of the horses at the back of the herd crash to the ground where it remained unmoving.

Father Casey made the sign of the cross as another shot echoed against the hillside and another horse fell to the ground.

Hap counted just twenty-nine horses, a number that indicated well over half the herd had already been slaughtered by the feds.

"Sir," shouted the BLM agent closest to Tuttle. "You need to move faster."

"He's right in the path of the horses," Father Casey said.

The priest might have been the only Savage resident watching the impending clash between the wild horses and an increasingly panicked Bill Tuttle with a sense of concern for Tuttle's well-being. Adeline Rhodes glanced up at Father Casey and then looked back down into the ravine, her words issued between clenched teeth.

"Good. I hope they trample the murdering bastard."

Tuttle fell once again and began rolling toward the ravine bottom. He cried out in terror as he saw the first of the remaining herd enter the ravine no more than a hundred yards away.

Hap's mouth twitched as he allowed himself a hint of satisfaction in watching how close Tuttle was to being trampled. He knew that normally a herd of horses would rarely run into a man but rather move itself to the side to avoid the impact. On this day, though, after hours of being chased and shot at, the horses were far beyond normal behavior. For them the morning had quite literally become a struggle of survival, a conflict brought about by the little man now wailing to be saved as he crouched in the middle of the ravine, his ears full of the herd's thunderous approach.

Tuttle lowered his head and shut his eyes tight while waving his hands out in front of him. The ground beneath him shook as the powerful creatures sped down the narrow path of the ravine.

Hap watched as the herd's alpha mare, a beautiful and powerful black and white female who had led the herd for the last seven years, appeared to lower her head and increase her speed even more as she neared Tuttle's cowering form.

At the last moment before impact the mare moved to the side so that just part of her front leg brushed against Tuttle's shoulder. That slight impact was still enough to send him sprawling backwards as his screams once again travelled up to everyone who stood watching from the top of the hill.

Adeline cursed softly under her breath, disappointed the mare had not ran Tuttle over.

The remaining herd copied the mare's example, shifting to the side of Tuttle and leaving him untouched, though the pounding fury of their passing left him babbling in terror.

259

Hap's entire body stiffened as the final member of the herd made its way toward Tuttle. It was the newly dominant stallion, a dark brown horse born just four springs ago but already a powerfully muscled beast that had quickly climbed to the top of the herd's social structure.

The rancher's keen eye noted how the stallion's movements indicated an injury to one of its hind legs. Its ears were pinned back against its head as it neared Tuttle, indicating the horse was in an extremely agitated state.

Probably has a wound somewhere around its hind quarters.

Hap's instincts were right. A bullet had grazed the middle portion of the horse's back left leg, tearing a path across its hock joint. The pain of the wound enraged the already naturally aggressive stallion.

At the very last moment before impact the horse bounded over the terrified Tuttle who opened his eyes in time to see the creature's dark belly soaring above him.

What Tuttle didn't see was the hoof at the end of the horse's injured leg as it crashed into the middle of his forehead. The force of the blow snapped Tuttle's neck and body backward and caused the lower portion of his skull to bounce with a wet crunch off a piece of jagged rock.

Everyone but Hap Wilkes winced at the sound.

Tuttle's body lay twisted and unmoving inside the ravine while the remaining horse herd sped off toward the Yellowstone River. Both BLM choppers momentarily circled above Tuttle's form before one touched down atop Vaughn's Hill and the other chopper sped off in the direction of Hap's home. The voice of the other agent who had been with Tuttle could be heard yelling into his phone that the BLM supervisor appeared to be dead.

Stan let out a long, low whistle. "Guess that's what people might call a big old serving of irony, huh?"

Hap looked over at his old friend and shook his head. The rancher's eyes gleamed with a satisfied light that reflected the bright Montana sun.

"No . . . I'd call that justice."

EPILOGUE 1

Bill Tuttle didn't actually die the day he attempted to wipe out an entire herd of wild horses.

That death came the following day.

Three weeks later the Bureau of Land Management concluded an investigation into the matter that found Tuttle might have possibly overstepped his authority but found no laws to have been broken. Since Tuttle was no longer available to either confirm or deny his part in the conflict the entire case was deemed closed and the records sealed.

Senator Burton Mansfield and his friends at Greenex were quite pleased by this outcome and quickly moved on to their next mutually beneficial project.

Two years later, Congressman Steve Moore ran against and defeated Senator Mansfield, forcing the longtime Washington D.C. fixture into unplanned retirement. An evaluation of the election results indicated Congressman Moore won 98% of the Richland County vote, a number that ultimately proved decisive in his victory over Burton Mansfield. Within the next year, Senator Moore successfully oversaw the termination of all federally funded projects to Greenex, a move that ultimately bankrupted the company.

Dillon Potts won his own re-election as Richland County Sheriff. More important to him, he also had several more opportunities to go fishing with his father Stan, whose health remained stable for another three years following the events on Vaughn's Hill.

It was two mornings after their last fishing trip that Stan Potts collapsed in the shower from a massive heart attack. Doctors told Dillon his father likely died almost immediately and so suffered very little.

At Stan's funeral, Hap Wilkes arrived and made certain to stop and speak with the sheriff. The rancher had become increasingly frail, his limp more pronounced, but the eyes remained bright and defiant and his grip firm and strong as he shook Dillon's hand.

"It was my honor to call your dad my friend. Stan Potts was a hell of a fine man who always put his family first."

The sheriff made certain to check in on Hap occasionally, each time worrying he would find the old rancher had passed on. Instead, Hap would glare back at the patrol car from his front porch and nod. It was the rancher's way of telling Dillon he was fine and to get the hell off his property.

Hap was not always alone, though. As months turned to years, Connor and Sarah made their way back to his ranch as often as their own increasingly busy lives would allow. Each visit would quietly remind the siblings Hap was growing weaker and they knew their grandfather's body had become a prison of near constant pain that made the simple act of getting out of bed in the morning a daunting task that left him exhausted.

That pain and his body's seemingly never-ending rebellion against itself had prevented the rancher from attending either of their weddings. Connor married first to a young woman he met during his final year of college. They moved to Portland, Oregon where Connor accepted a position as a technician for a music production studio.

Like Connor, Sarah met her future husband in college as well and moved with him to a sprawling desert ranch property twenty minutes outside of Palm Springs. She came to inherit the same love of horses both her grandmother and grandfather had shared. Sarah and her husband started a trail riding company catering to the wealthy Palm Springs clientele, a business that soon proved both profitable and enjoyable.

It was a visit by Sarah nearly six years after she had first arrived at his ranch that provided Hap the determination to make certain he hung on just a little bit longer. Sarah sat down with her grandfather in his living room and told him she was four months pregnant with her first child.

Hap sat momentarily stunned by how quickly time had moved around him. Sarah had entered his life as a teenaged girl but was now a young married woman running her own business and preparing to be a mother. The rancher grinned and shook his head as she took his hands into her own.

"After I have the baby, I'm going to come visit you, Grandpa, okay?"

Hap understood Sarah's true meaning. She was telling him to stick around long enough to see his first great-grandchild. He looked at her and nodded.

"Don't worry. I'll still be here. I promise."

Keeping that promise proved tougher than Hap ever intended it to be. A month before Sarah gave birth he fell in the kitchen and remained on the floor for two days. He might have died there if not for a visit from Dillon who called medics and had the rancher transported to the hospital in Sydney where doctors

265

quickly diagnosed him with a broken hip and placed him in surgery the following day.

Hap returned home three days after surgery following an expletive-drenched tirade where he demanded to be released. He was driven back to Savage by the sheriff who couldn't help but be amused at how much fight still remained in the old rancher.

"You still know how to give 'em hell, Hap."

Hap merely grunted. He was in no mood to talk.

Once home he worked hard to regain as much mobility as possible in preparation for Sarah's next visit. This took the help of a walker which allowed Hap to move about his home on his own, albeit very slowly. The sheriff took to checking in on Hap every day and though the rancher's outward mood appeared annoyed by his regular presence, he knew Hap appreciated the company. Something foreign had crept into the rancher's eyes—fear.

Hap knew death was more determined than ever to take him and he worried it would happen before he saw his great-grandchild. Nights were the worst. He would lie in his bed looking up at the ceiling, unable to close his eyes, thinking they might not open again. When sleep finally came it was fragmented into various and increasingly vivid dreams.

One of those dreams was a conversation with his grandfather. Vaughn Wilkes sat looking at Hap from the same chair January had tried to sell all those years ago. He appeared as Hap had always remembered him: a long and lean face, friendly green eyes, and silver remnants of what had once been a full head of reddish-brown hair.

"You look ready, Hap."

The rancher knew Vaughn was speaking of dying so he ignored the comment. Vaughn chuckled softly as he lit his ever-present pipe and then blew a large cloud of sweet-smelling tobacco smoke into the space between Hap and himself.

"Fair enough. We don't need to talk about that. You know . . . I've met him."

Hap went ahead and allowed himself to be drawn into his grandfather's purposely open-ended comment. "Who?"

Vaughn's eyes twinkled, knowing he had his grandson's interest. "Your son, Dex."

Hap turned himself slowly toward the kitchen, moving the walker away from his grandfather while answering him with his back turned. "That's not possible. You died long before Dex was born."

The rancher again heard his grandfather's soft, low chuckle. "Stop being so stubborn, Hap. You know how it's possible. You should take comfort in knowing just about *anything* is possible from where I'm sitting."

Hap took a deep breath and closed his eyes. "This isn't real. I'm dreaming is all—just the silly dreams of an old man."

"Don't disrespect me, young man. You know better. If this was just a dream, then why do you still need that walker to get around?"

Hap shrugged. "Hell if I know. Why are you here? If it's to take me with you, I'm not going. Not yet. I still have a promise to keep. I gave my word."

The rancher could hear his grandfather getting up out of the chair behind him. He didn't turn around, fearing he would have no choice but to leave with Vaughn to whatever place dead men went to when life was finished with them.

"Yes, Hap, I know how important your word is to you, just like I know how important it is to see your great-grandchild.

Don't worry. I won't be the one to guide you. She made certain she would be the one doing that."

Hap lifted his face upward as his nose detected a familiar and cherished memory.

It was the unmistakable scent of Chanel.

Sarah arrived at the ranch three months after that dream holding her newborn child in her arms as she walked toward Hap who proudly stood on his front porch without the aid of the walker. He saw Sarah's eyes widen when she first saw him and knew his weakened appearance alarmed her. She recovered quickly, though, and was soon smiling again as she turned to show off her baby to her grandfather.

"Grandpa Hap, I want to introduce you to your great-grandson."

Hap's hands trembled as he carefully took the child into his arms. The baby's eyes looked into his, generations linked by blood, actions, consequences, and fate. He was unable to speak as he stared back into the face of his great-grandson, overcome by their shared past, present, and future.

"What's his name?"

"We named him after my dad. Grandpa Hap, this is Dex."

The impact of hearing that name as he held the newborn jolted the old rancher, breaking through the emotional wall behind which he hid those things in his life he did not wish to be reminded of. Hap's mouth opened, but he found himself unable to speak. He did not have the words to express the simultaneous pain and joy of holding Sarah's son, a child given the name of his own son who, by self-imposed omission, the rancher had never come to know.

Sarah and Dex stayed the night at the ranch and then left the following morning with Hap promising repeatedly that he would take care of himself. Sarah must have told her brother of her concerns for him because a few hours after she left Connor called on the cell phone he had given Hap as a Christmas gift two years earlier.

Connor chatted for a few minutes about his work and a fishing trip he was planning next week and then told Hap he was hoping to be out to the ranch in June with his wife who was due to give birth to their first child in September. He told Hap he looked forward to being able to show him his second great-grandchild next year.

Hap said he was looking forward to that as well even as he silently admitted to himself the probability of being around long enough to do so was unlikely. When a pause entered the conversation, Connor took the opportunity to tell Hap something he had wanted to share with him for some time.

"Grandpa, I wanted to say how much my getting to know you has meant to me. I love you."

Hap smiled into the phone, temporarily feeling the ever-present weight of regret lift itself from off his shoulders. "Thank you, Connor. You're a good man and you're going to be a wonderful father. I love you, too."

That evening, Hap eased himself into bed feeling bone-tired yet also content. His life, while terribly imperfect, had managed to help create some measure of good and as the night's darkness enveloped the bedroom, and growing fatigue pushed his eyes closed, he allowed himself a little smile as the world around him went silent.

EPILOGUE 2

Hap awoke to the sound of Dog barking from outside.

What has got him so riled up?

He pushed himself out of bed and quickly dressed. Soon he was standing on his porch in the cool air of a Montana spring night.

"Dog!"

More barking sounded from near the barn. Hap jogged to where he believed he would find the dog but again he was unable to locate him. He yelled for Dog once again and was rewarded with yet more barking. The animal sounded urgent but not frightened—almost playful. Dog was now moving quickly through the field toward Vaughn's Hill.

A familiar sigh issued from inside the barn. Peanut stood there already saddled, patiently waiting for Hap to begin the ride. The rancher ran his hands along her neck and scratched behind her ear.

Peanut turned her head to nudge him back toward her side, a move Hap knew was her way of letting him know she was anxious to get going. The rancher lifted his left foot into the stirrup and easily swung himself smoothly into the saddle, the place he felt himself born to be.

"Okay girl, let's go see what old Dog is up to."

Peanut trotted swiftly toward the field as Dog barked yet again a hundred yards or so ahead. Hap leaned forward while his face broke out into a wide grin as he squeezed his heals against Peanut's sides.

"Yaaahhhh!"

The horse catapulted herself forward, breaking out into a full gallop. Hap matched his movements in the saddle to the motion of Peanut's body as she sped across the field. His grin widened as the welcome sting of cool wind whipped across his face while Dog ran between the tall grass just ahead of them.

Just try to keep up old man.

Hap's head turned at the sound of Shirley's voice.

Peanut arrived at the base of Vaughn's Hill and began the ascent to the top. Dog's barking sounded even more urgent. Hap could see a hint of the sunrise that was emerging from the east.

Hurry, Hap. I promise you're almost home. What could have been will now be forever. God doesn't punish. God is love and love is everything.

After getting to the top of Vaughn's Hill Hap found himself looking at the small ranch home he had just left, though, it was no longer suffering from years of neglect and falling apart. Warm light shined through its windows. He breathed in the smell of breakfast being cooked.

Dog sat on the porch wagging his tail and looking back at Hap as if he couldn't actually believe it took the rancher that long to finally get there. Peanut walked to the porch and then waited for Hap to dismount.

The sound of singing came from inside the home, followed by the laughter of a child. Hap paused with his foot hovering over the first porch step, hesitating to go inside.

He realized then that his hesitation came not out of fear but rather because of his own guilt.

This can't be for me. I don't deserve this.

Behind him, the sun broke across the landscape, its eternal light gently pushing back the darkness.

Hap slowly moved his hand toward the door, feeling the cool metal of the handle on his skin, followed by the loving voice of Shirley greeting him.

There's my Irish cowboy.

Hap opened the door.

A young boy shouted with delight at his arrival, running from the kitchen with his small arms outstretched. The boy's mother looked up and smiled back at Hap. Husband and wife shared an unspoken moment of contentment for the life they had chosen to spend together.

Hap hugged Dex close to him as Shirley crossed the room to then wrap her arms tightly around both father and son.

Hello, Hap.

Shirley had kept her promise.

Hap Wilkes was finally home.

———

Note: Please remember to leave a review for *The Irish Cowboy* on its Amazon book page.

And if you enjoyed *The Irish Cowboy*, be sure to check out *SAVAGE* by D.W. Ulsterman as well.

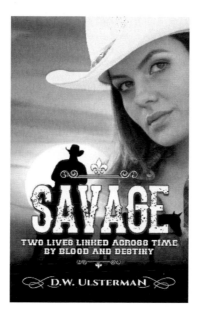

ABOUT THE AUTHOR

D.W. Ulsterman is the writer of the Kindle Scout-winning *San Juan Islands Mystery* series published by Kindle Press as well as the #1 bestselling family dramas, *The Irish Cowboy* and *Savage*.

He lives with his wife of 26 years in the Pacific Northwest. During the summer months you can find him navigating the waters of his beloved San Juan Islands on his trawler, 'Liberty Belle'. He is the proud father of two grown children and is also best friends with Dublin the Dobe.

Made in United States
North Haven, CT
22 February 2022

16383898R00169